SOME STORIES ARE NOT SEEN

MINDY HARDWICK

EAGLE BAY PRESS

Eagle Bay Press

PRINT ISBN: 978-0-578-84781-8
First Edition: April 2021

Developmental Editor: Sarah Cloots
Copy Editor: Monique Conrod
Cover Artist: Su Kopil, Earthly Charms
Book Format and Layout: Eagle Bay Press

Eagle Bay Press
P.O. Box 1391
Cannon Beach, Oregon. 97110

For the Haystack Rock Awareness Program

ACKNOWLEDGMENTS

This story was inspired during the three seasons I volunteered as an environmental interpreter for the Haystack Rock Awareness Program in Cannon Beach, Oregon. The Haystack Rock Awareness Program is a stewardship and environmental education program whose mission is to protect, through education, the intertidal and bird ecology of the Marine Garden and Oregon Island National Wildlife Refuge at Haystack Rock. The jewelry Lucy makes in her STEAM club is based on the Trash Talk program started by Haystack Rock Awareness Outreach Coordinator, Pooka Rice. To learn more about the Haystack Rock Awareness Program please visit their website: https://www.ci.cannon-beach.or.us/hrap

Thank you to the amazing women who inspired this story through their dedication and passion for the Haystack Rock Awareness Program (HRAP) during the three years I volunteered with HRAP: Lisa Habecker, Haystack Rock Awareness Program Education Coordinator; Pooka Rice, HRAP Outreach Coordinator; Kari Henningsgaard, HRAP Communications Coordinator; Melissa Keyser, Haystack Rock

Awareness Program Coordinator; Andrea Suarez, HRAP Bilingual Interpreter; Briana Ortega, whose companionship and earmuffs on HRAP shifts always made me smile on the cold rainy days; and Jacie Gregory, who educated me about both the tide pools and birds on the beach, as well as teenage life in the halls of Seaside High School.

During the writing of this story, I spent a year and a half substitute teaching on the North Oregon Coast and I'd like to give a special shout-out to the elementary teachers at Astor Elementary and Lewis and Clark Elementary in Astoria, Oregon, Warrenton Grade School in Warrenton, Oregon, and Gearhart Elementary in Seaside, Oregon, whose classrooms provided insight and inspiration for this story. A special thank you to Literary Arts in Portland who, during COVID-19, provided funding to me from the Booth Emergency Fund.

COTTAGES FOR RENT

*M*om and I moved around a lot. Sometimes we slept in hotel rooms with thin covers and the sound of TVs floating through the walls. Other times we rented one-bedroom apartments, slept on the floor on blow-up mattresses and cooked with our box of thrift store kitchen utensils.

But I hoped all that moving around was going to stop when Mom drove our used Ford Taurus past the wooden sign on Highway 105, with the white lettering that read "Sea Rock Cove." Tall evergreens framed the two-lane highway which stretched along the Oregon Coast. Sea Rock Cove was ninety miles west of Portland, Oregon, where Mom and I had been living. It was four hours south of Seattle where I was born. But most importantly, Sea Rock Cove was where Dad grew up.

It was a cloudy Saturday morning in April. Light sprinkles of rain dotted Mom's windshield, but not enough that she had to turn on the wipers, which always left streaks across the glass because they needed to be replaced. A huge basalt

Haystack Rock loomed out of the ocean ahead of us. I fingered the small, silver sea star I wore on the chain around my neck. Dad had given me the necklace and it matched the tattoo on his left arm. I bounced my left leg up and down. I was finally going to see the sea stars Dad had always talked about before he died.

Dad said he wanted to be a marine biologist, but it took a lot of school and he didn't have the patience for school. So, he worked on a fishing boat in Alaska which took him out to sea. Then he met Mom while he was docked in Seattle. After I was born, Mom didn't want Dad to be gone six months at a time, so he tried to get an office job. The problem was, Dad wasn't really an office person and the jobs never lasted long, so we moved around a lot chasing the next job.

A herd of elk chomped grass along the side of the curvy exit road. Mom didn't slow the car until we screeched to a stop at a four-way stop sign. We were the only car at the intersection, and I was pretty sure we could have flown through and no one would have noticed.

The small box on my lap slid toward my knees and I placed my arms around it. I had learned how to carry my science box when Mom drove. I never packed it in the back seat, where it might crash to the floor in a quick stop and my specimen jars would land in a broken heap.

Mom glanced at a yellow sticky attached to the dashboard and steered the car straight into a small downtown area. At 8:00 a.m., the shingled, storybook galleries, small restaurants, ice cream and candy store, boutique clothing stores, pet store and library hadn't opened yet. Mom drove up a small hill and the Haystack Rock, called Sea Rock, loomed even closer on my left. There were lots of these rock formations all along the Oregon Coast. They were carved out of the coastline by the wind and waves and eroded into interesting shapes. A few of them got the name Haystack Rock because they looked like piles of hay. But I didn't think Sea Rock looked anything like a haystack. I rolled down the window. The seagulls' cries filled the air and the salty scent of the ocean wafted through the town like the smell of cotton candy at a fair.

We drove past a wood-shingled building with peaks and arches that made it look like a small castle. The two-story building leaned a bit to the left and the porch steps were at a slight angle. A painting of Sea Rock hung in the middle of a front window. A thin, white-haired man sat on the porch in a wooden chair, his feet propped on a red stool, a blanket draped over his legs and a cup of coffee in his hands. He studied an easel in front of him that held a half-painted canvas. The man didn't look up as we drove by. I hoped people in Sea Rock Cove were friendly, like the people in the house-less car camps where we had been staying.

Mom checked the address again and slowed her speed as she drove past shingle-sided one-and two-story summer cottages—most of which were empty. Occasionally a small lamp glowed through a window in the cloudy morning and showed yellow painted walls with beach scene paintings or family photos. She stopped at Evergreen Avenue to turn left. A man on a bike swerved in front of us from the other direction. He carried a large, army-green sack over his shoulder, and a black dog, about the size of a Lab, ran alongside him. He grinned and waved.

I stuck my arm out the window and waved back, glad to see the town did have at least one friendly person.

Mom drove down a gravel road and stopped in front of six small, brown, vacation rental cottages with a worn sign in front: The Villas at Sea Rock Cove. Each small building was more a one-bedroom cottage than a fancy villa, with a faded blue door and a sea star with a number in it centered on the door. A couple of flowerpots perched outside the cottage doors with nothing growing in them. A small, ranch-style house with a sign that read "Office" sat at the back of the U-shaped cluster of cottages.

"This is it, Mom," I said. "Home."

We had never stayed in one place long enough to call anywhere home. My favorite "home" had been a rustic lodge tucked into the Cascade Range of Washington State. I'd spent long afternoons exploring the woods and trails, collecting everything from mossy specimens to slugs to wet leaves. But Mom and Dad's job managing a small hotel ended with a wildfire that took out everything in its path, including Dad. After Dad died, Mom's jobs seemed to all be in the cities. Her last job, working in a fancy hotel in downtown Portland, hadn't paid enough for us to rent anything in Portland, and we had been living in our car in a camp with six other car-home families for the last two months.

A fat brown bunny hopped across the overgrown yard toward a rusted bike with a wicker basket. "Aunt Charlotte said the keys are over the door," Mom said.

Aunt Charlotte was Dad's older sister by ten years, and because they didn't have a mom when they were growing up, Dad said she was always bossing him around. Dad didn't like her very much. I had only met her once, when we lived in Seattle. She was attending a big real estate conference and we met her for pizza at Pioneer Square. Aunt Charlotte complained the whole time about the people begging for money. Dad sometimes played in a jazz band in Pioneer Square and knew some of the guys who hung out during the day on the benches. His jaw did that funny thing and he never ate a bite of his pizza. We didn't see Aunt Charlotte again.

Aunt Charlotte called once a week, though, always on Sundays, and sent me presents for Christmas and my birthday.

Sometimes the presents didn't catch up with us for months as they followed our change-of-address notices. Mom never returned Aunt Charlotte's calls. Until last week.

Aunt Charlotte owned a real estate company in Sea Rock Cove and said she knew of rental cottages that needed a new manager. The job came with its own living quarters. Aunt Charlotte said it was a great job because long-term housing was scarce in the town due to the massive amounts of vacation homes and second homes. Mom didn't tell her that housing was scarce with us too, but she called her right back and took the job.

The light spring rain sprinkled across the windshield as Mom popped the trunk. I opened the passenger door and stepped around a white bunny munching on grass. A light brown bunny eyed me from beside the middle cottage and a black bunny dashed across the patio of the fourth cottage.

"What's with the bunnies?" I hoisted my box of journals, glass jars, gloves and small dissection kit out of the car.

"Mmm? The rabbits?" Mom opened the trunk and turned as a white bunny hopped across the yard.

"They look like pets." Pet bunnies were snow white. The rabbits we saw in the woods when we camped on old logging trails were always brown, and bigger. "Do the cottages have pet bunnies like a petting zoo?"

Mom frowned. "Aunt Charlotte didn't say anything about pet bunnies."

I counted five bunnies before I reached the front door of the small house with its rusted door handle. I waited for Mom to set our box of bedding on the ground before she stood on her tiptoes and grabbed a key that had been left on top of the wooden door frame.

Mom inserted the key, turned the knob and stepped inside. I followed her and inhaled. The house smelled damp and musty. A red and brown couch sat in the middle of the room, with a matching chair and a brown, scratched wooden table. I placed my science box on the floor by the couch. The jars inside rattled against the small notebooks where I recorded my scientific findings.

A bookcase full of books rested along the back wall. I stepped closer to the bookcase and scanned the titles. Coffee table books about the ocean, and books about surfing. A thin layer of dust covered the middle and bottom shelves, and I ran my finger through the dust in a wavy line. Field guides to birds, sea life and the flora of the Pacific Northwest. Books about lighthouses, and the lives of octopuses. I pulled out a thick book, *Between Pacific Tides* by Edward F. Ricketts and Jack Calvin. I knew the black and white drawings by heart. I had borrowed the book from a Seattle library and studied the pages for hours. I copied the drawings into my logbooks along with detailed notes about each species found in tide pools along the Pacific Coast.

Tucked among the other books was a battered copy of *The Sea of Cortez* by John Steinbeck.

I swallowed hard.

"Lucy?" Mom peered over my shoulders.

"Dad's favorite book." I ran my finger over the scratched cover and the tear in the right corner. Mom kept all of Dad's things in a box. She never unpacked the box because she said it was easier to move and not forget something by mistake. We didn't talk much about Dad since he died two years ago, but sometimes I found her, at night, with a glass of wine, pulling out each item and running her hands over the books, a couple of old t-shirts and his favorite winter scarf.

Mom squeezed my shoulder. "Don't dwell on anything too long," she always said. Mom opened a small hall closet. A broom, mop and bucket fell out, along with a small mouse that scurried across the hardwood floor and out the open door.

"I think this place needs a good clean." Mom wiped her forehead. "I hope the cottages are in better shape, but somehow I've afraid they won't be." She smiled at me warily. "You ready for this, Lucy?"

"Sure." I hugged Mom. How could I not be? We were in Dad's town. The place where he had grown up. The place where he had first fallen in love with sea stars. Somewhere in this town were not only the sea stars but also the people who had known Dad when he was twelve like me.

I hopped away from Mom. I couldn't wait to explore the beach and find Dad's sea stars. I would become the marine biologist Dad always wanted to be, in the town where he had lived. It seemed like destiny to me. I was more than ready!

SEA ROCK COVE

A few hours later, the house smelled like vinegar, the dust and cobwebs were swept away, and the wood floors shone. The early morning marine layer clouds had broken up into puffy white clouds in a blue sky. Mom sat working at a small desk by the door. I dumped the last bucket of dirty water onto the grassy area by the back door. A faded blue one-speed bike leaned against the left corner of the house. A little bit of rust dotted the spokes but otherwise it seemed in good condition. I dropped the bucket and hollered into the doorway at Mom. "Can I use this bike?"

"Mmmm …" Mom barely lifted her head. It would be hours before she finished setting up new utility accounts and reading through cottage reservations. Not to mention she had to figure out where our nearest walk out of town was in case of a tsunami. Beside Mom sat a stack of plastic signs that told guests which way to walk toward high ground and what to do in case of a tsunami. Each one had to be attached to the back of the door of every cottage. Dad always explained how a lot of people thought tsunamis only happened in Japan, but they also happen along the West Coast of the United States. In 1964, a big earthquake in Alaska triggered a tsunami wave of thirty feet in Sea Rock Cove that took out a bridge on the north end and knocked homes off their foundations. After that, the people of Sea Rock Cove didn't mess around with the possibility of tsunamis. Once a month, the town tested a warning system that sounded from speakers located all over town, and people could practice walking their route to high ground safety. The practice warning system sounded like a cow mooing so people would know it was a practice drill. In a real tsunami, the alert was a siren. I hoped we'd never hear the real siren.

I grabbed my backpack from a small hook by the door and adjusted the strap against my shoulder, making sure not to rattle the three glass canning jars. There were a lot of things I needed to study if I wanted to be a marine biologist. I hoped to fill each jar with an animal from the tide pools that I could label with the scientific name and record in my notebook. I had cleared a nice space on the window ledge in my new bedroom to place all the filled jars. I grabbed the bike handlebars and steered the bike onto the gravel road.

A cold breeze blew across my face. I dove deeper into my oversized sweatshirt and pedaled hard. In Portland, spring was warm, and I wore short-sleeve shirts without a sweatshirt. The cottage yards I passed bloomed with tulips and colorful pink and white rhododendrons. Even though it was Saturday, almost all of the cottages had closed blinds and drapes. Two cottages had small circular signs attached to the front: Beach Vacation Rental. It looked like the rental season hadn't quite started yet.

I pedaled onto the town's main road and made sure to stay on the sidewalk on the few blocks to the downtown area. Aunt Charlotte's real estate office was in a cluster of shops with a high-end boutique clothing store, a shop that sold beach-themed linens and a flower shop. Each storefront had the same cedar shingles I'd seen on all the cottages. The whole town looked like something out of one of those holiday movies Mom liked to watch, where the couples always had a happily ever after.

I pedaled past the building that looked like a miniature castle with its spiked roofline. The painting of Sea Rock filled the front window. There were colorful purple and orange sea stars painted along the bottom of the mammoth Sea Rock. The sea stars looked just like Dad had described them! A small wooden Closed sign hung across the door, but I was sure I saw the man's narrow face peer through the upstairs window. I picked up my pace and pedaled faster.

In another two blocks, I slowed as I rode past The Bow Wow Beach Dog shop window. Colorful cut-out bones with the names of pets and their owners who had donated to the local animal shelter lined the front windows. If I had a dog, one of the first things I would do is go into that shop. I wanted a dog, but Mom said our life was too much in motion and it was too hard to find a pet-friendly place to rent.

Music floated down the street and I followed the sound to a tall, thin man standing in front of a restaurant with open patio seating. He wore faded blue jeans with a rip in the left pant leg. A too-big flannel shirt hung open over a well-worn grey t-shirt that said Pluto's Books in light blue letters. His tennis shoes had holes in the sides, the same way tennis shoes did that I saw at the thrift stores. It was the same man I had seen on the bike. The dog lay by his side and an open guitar case with a few dollar bills lying inside was in front of him. His bike leaned against a bush and peeking out of the bush was a green duffle bag, as if he had tried to position the bike to hide the duffle bag. In Portland and Seattle, I saw a lot of people that looked like this man, but they always had a cardboard sign that said *Help Please. Food or Money,* which lay beside them on busy street corners.

I recognized the song as one Mom liked to sing. It was something from the '70s; folksy and blues-ish at the same time.

I pulled my bike up beside him. His dog eyed me from his perch on a clean flannel blanket, but he didn't make a move toward me. "Can I pet your dog?"

The man stopped singing but kept playing his guitar. "She doesn't like most people."

The dog's sides were filled out and she wore a nice red collar with Sea Rock Cove stitched in blue lettering. A rabies tag dangled from the collar. I didn't see a tag that said where she lived like most dogs. But, she seemed like a well-kept dog. The dog's clear dark eyes peered back at me.

"I'll be right back." I leaned my bike against the stone wall and walked to the Bow Wow Beach Dog shop.

I opened the door and a small bell tinkled above my head. "Do you have something for the dog outside?" A rack of fancy dog collars and leashes stood beside a big stuffed dog. I bet the real dogs peed on the stuffed one.

The woman walked to a deep refrigerator at the back of the store. She wore dark blue jeans and a heavy grey sweatshirt with The Bow Wow Beach Dog Shop etched across the middle in white letters and a picture of two dogs running on the beach. The woman pulled out a raw bone and handed it to me.

"How much is it?" I only had a $1.50 that I had found tucked into the crevices of a beat-up leather couch at a coffee shop Mom and I had stopped at before we left Portland.

"That's okay." She brushed her hand at me in a dismissive motion. "It's on me."

"Thanks!" I hollered over my shoulder as I headed back out the door. I would be sure to return to this dog shop. The cottages accepted dogs and I would tell all the guests to make sure they took their dog to the Bow Wow Beach Dog shop!

"I have something for your dog." I showed the man the dog bone.

"Luna will like that," he said, and grinned at me. Even though his clothes looked a little dirty, his teeth were straight and even. They looked cleaner than mine. I hadn't been to the dentist in a while. The last time we went it was one of those free clinics. I guess free meant they told you that you had a lot of cavities to fill. By the time we left I didn't think I had a tooth without a filling. Mom said I was exaggerating, and it had only been two.

I squatted beside Luna and laid the treat for her on the blanket. She sniffed it and gingerly moved her tongue over the bone. She wagged her tail.

"That'll keep her busy for a while." The man stuck out his hand. "I'm Thomas."

"I'm Lucy," I said. "I just moved to town. My mom is managing the cottages over there." I waved my hand back toward where I had just come from. "My dad grew up here."

"Who is your dad?" Thomas's blue eyes shone in his weather-worn face. More than one wrinkle lined his forehead and alongside his jaw. He looked like he could be close to how old Dad should have been.

"Rick Lavender," I said. "Did you know him?"

Thomas nodded. "He was a couple years ahead of me in school. We used to climb Sea Rock together."

"You can climb Sea Rock?" I wanted to climb Sea Rock! I bet there were a lot of great things to study on the top of that big rock!

"Nope." Thomas strummed his guitar. "It's a National

Wildlife Refuge. Everything above the high tide line is part of the protection zone for the birds who nest and live there, and can't be climbed or walked on. But people used to try sometimes."

"What happened?" I asked. I could just see Dad climbing Sea Rock. He would make it all the way to the top!

"If they catch you," Thomas said, and paused, "you can get a big fine or go to jail. We didn't get that far. It was winter and pouring rain. We figured no one was going to really see us too well. But we barely got into the saddle of the rock, the lower part, before we decided it wasn't a good idea. The rain was just too strong in our faces for us to do much climbing."

"Wow!" I said. "Dad never told me that story." It sounded like a great adventure. Why hadn't Dad told me the story? Did he think I was too young? I was ten when he died. I could have handled the climbing story.

Thomas shrugged. "Not all stories are told."

"Dad told me he wanted to be a marine biologist," I said, wanting Thomas to know that Dad did tell me some important things about himself. "But he died and now I'm going to be one."

"I'm sorry about your dad." Thomas strummed chords on his guitar. "I think I heard something had happened to him a few years ago. Your grandpa told me, I think."

"I don't have a grandpa." I crossed my hands over my chest. Dad and Mom always said it was just us. Dad's parents were both dead and Mom's parents had retired in Florida—way too far away for us to visit when we barely had any money, and they had a retirement income that didn't allow for much traveling either. I talked to them on the phone sometimes, but that was about it.

Thomas played a loud chord. The sound seemed to reverberate everywhere. "You don't have a grandpa?" He repeated my words slowly.

"No." I shook my head and stuck my hands in my pockets. I guess Thomas didn't know Dad so well after all. "Dad said Grandpa died in a car accident before I was born. Dad has a sister, Aunt Charlotte, who lives in Sea Rock Cove." I puckered my lips. "But Dad didn't like her very much so we only saw her once. She got Mom the job at the cottages."

Thomas eyed me and his eyebrow arched. "Charlotte owns the real estate company. I know her." He continued to play his guitar but his strong chords had moved into a mellow tune. "Sea Rock Cove is a good place to land. Always good to get to know your family."

I wasn't going to tell Thomas, but I didn't think Mom and I were going to get to know Aunt Charlotte very well. It might be harder to avoid her weekly Sunday calls in Sea Rock Cove, where she could pop over to see us, but I doubted Mom would want us to spend a lot of time with her. "Your Dad would have preferred it this way," Mom would say. She said that a lot, especially about Aunt Charlotte.

"Do you have a favorite song?" Thomas strummed his guitar. "I can play lots of things. I was going to be a musician but it didn't work out so well."

I told him the name of a song Mom liked to sing when we drove in the car for a long time. He immediately began playing. "That's an old favorite."

Thomas hadn't finished the song when across the street Aunt Charlotte hurried out of the post office. "Lucy!"

"Uh oh," I rolled my eyes. It was happening already. The small town can't-get-away-from-each-other syndrome. Dad had talked about it and said he left Sea Rock Cove because it was just too small for him. Even though he loved the ocean, he said there were plenty of other bodies of water and he didn't need to go back to Sea Rock Cove and be under a microscope again. Mom always said it was just part of his wandering feet.

Aunt Charlotte motioned for me to cross the street. She shifted her large, fancy designer leather bag onto her left shoulder. I didn't have to look to know that inside was the most recent model of a laptop with all the latest apps uploaded, and probably a matching cell phone stuck in an outside pocket. Women who dressed like Aunt Charlotte always had those things. Mom and I never had a computer and always had to use the library ones. Mom got a cell phone at one of the shelters for houseless women and children. But it was about three versions behind the current models.

"I guess I better go," I said to Thomas. I didn't want to talk to Aunt Charlotte, but I couldn't be rude. She had gotten Mom and me the job, and she *was* family. "Nice to meet you."

"Nice to meet you." Thomas kept playing my song and Luna chewed on the bone. "Thanks for the dog treat. We'll see you around."

"See you around." I hoped to see a lot more of Thomas and Luna. If I couldn't have a dog, then maybe I could share Luna.

I hopped on my bike and, looking both ways, crossed the street.

"What were you doing?" Aunt Charlotte frowned at me. She wore khaki cropped pants and a light blue cardigan sweater over a matching blouse and smelled like a really expensive perfume, which made my stomach feel queasy.

"Talking to Thomas," I said. "And Luna, his dog. Thomas said Dad tried to climb Sea Rock in high school."

Aunt Charlotte looked away from me and across the street. She played with a pearl and turquoise beaded key ring which hung from one silver hook of her bag strap, moving it between her fingers. Her nails were the special kind of nails

15

that women had to get fixed every week. "I forgot about the rock-climbing story."

"He also said my grandpa is still living, but I set him straight."

Aunt Charlotte stared at me with a piercing stare. Her eyes were the same hazel color as Dad's. "I don't think spending time with Thomas is a very good idea."

"But, he knew Dad!" He had remembered a story about Dad that Aunt Charlotte had forgotten. What other stories had Aunt Charlotte forgotten about Dad?

"Mmm." Aunt Charlotte pursed her lips in that way grown-ups had when you were doing something they didn't think was a good idea. "There are children your age who live here. I'll see if I can find some for you to meet. You'll start school on Monday, so I'm sure there will be people your age to play with."

I swayed back and forth with my feet planted on the ground and my bike moving between my legs. I didn't want to be ungrateful to Aunt Charlotte for helping us, but I didn't want her to find me friends either. I had just turned twelve. We didn't have playdates like children. Why did grown-ups always think they were being helpful? I stared past Aunt Charlotte at the shingled building with Library written in white across a sign in the middle of the door. "I'm going to explore in the library. I want to research some marine animals."

"What a bright girl you are!" Aunt Charlotte said. "I'll go see how your Mom is doing. I'd love for us to all have dinner together a couple times a week now that you are here." She squeezed my shoulder. "I can't wait to get to know you better!" Her perfume circled so heavily around me I thought I might gag. Maybe Aunt Charlotte had never married because she wore too much perfume and smelled bad.

"Okay," I muttered and kicked my feet against my pedals.

Despite what Thomas said about getting to know your family, I wasn't sure I wanted to get to know Aunt Charlotte better. She seemed like those women who tried to help Mom and me, with their soft smiles and sympathy-pooled eyes, who dished out soup and opened clothing closets to us at the churches on winter nights. Mom always parked far away from their expensive cars in the parking lot. "We've just fallen on hard times. We'll get back on our feet," she said.

I turned around to wave at Thomas, but he didn't see me. He poured water from a small container into Luna's bowl. After Luna finished, Thomas stuffed the dog dish inside the green duffle bag tucked under the bush. This time, I could see two other bags lying alongside the wall of the restaurant. The bags looked like the ones I'd seen men carrying and storing behind bushes and shrubs when Mom and I lived in the car camp. Was Thomas houseless? I knew that things happened and people didn't stay in their homes where they grew up, but all those empty cottages with the nice yards…Surely Thomas must have somewhere to live in Sea Rock Cove.

Thomas hiked up his too-big pants, reached into his bag and grabbed a small rope and slipped it through the belt loops. Luna waited by his side. I made a note to ask the nice lady at the Bow Wow Beach Dog shop how to get a tag for Luna with her home and Thomas's phone number on it. All dogs should have a tag with a home address in case they got lost.

3
FIELD TRIP

*O*n Monday, Mom pulled into the gravel parking lot of Pelican Elementary School, a long, rectangular red building with windows that stretched the entire length of the school and overlooked a grassy sports field. Three portables clustered beside the school. Aunt Charlotte had told us how Sea Rock Cove used to have an elementary school, but it had been built in the tsunami zone and the school district closed it a few years ago. Now, all the Sea Rock Cove elementary kids traveled fifteen minutes up the highway to the next town, Pelican Shores, to go to school. The middle and high schools had always been in Pelican Shores.

The good thing about the coast schools is they were small with only a few hundred kids so it would be easy to find my way around, unlike the one I had been attending in Portland where I'd gotten lost the first day of school and an eighth grade level counselor found me sniffling, just a little, in the hallway outside the gymnasium.

"I think that's the middle school." I pointed to a similar red building tucked alongside tall evergreens whose towering green branches swayed in the wind. My stomach fluttered and I swallowed, trying to move saliva into my dry mouth. I hated first days of school. And I had to do a lot of them.

Mom shook her head. A strand of brown hair escaped her scrunchie and she pushed it off her forehead. "The school district said to register you at Pelican Elementary School."

"Okay." I shrugged and wiped my palms along the sides of my too-big jeans. Unless the portables were middle school classrooms, there must be some mistake. Sixth grade was in a middle school. I tried to take a deep breath like one of the counselors had taught us in fifth grade. "Take deep breaths," she said. "It will calm you. Talk to yourself positively. You are capable." At the time it seemed funny and the whole class had laughed.

But now her message seemed like a key to settling my racing thoughts. *I am capable.* I repeated the words silently to myself. Mom and I would walk into the elementary school office and they would take a look at me and tell us we were at the wrong school. I could dash through the trees to the middle school and still have enough time to get into my first period class before I had to walk into a classroom filled with staring sixth graders who would easily find a new girl way more interesting than a morning journal warm-up routine. I knew the ritual well and I hoped to avoid it every time I had to start a new school.

Mom parked the car in a space marked "Visitor."

Showtime.

I hefted my backpack to my shoulders and followed Mom up two flights of stairs and into an open lobby with a big cafeteria just beyond. The smell of chlorine cleaning supplies mixed with cooked eggs hit me square in the face and I tried not to gag.

Mom turned left and we stepped into a small room with a

large counter. My legs felt like soft sand that could cascade out from beneath me at any minute. Behind the counter, two teachers who looked to be in their twenties poured coffee and scooped mail out of the teacher mail boxes with cheerful little labels.

I stepped up to the counter and leaned against it. "Hi," I said to a dark-haired lady wearing a purple scoop t-shirt. Pelican Elementary School was printed in white letters across the front and a pelican swooped between the words. She looked about Mom's age, mid-thirties or so, and dark circles rimmed her jet-black eyes. "I'm Lucy Lavender and this is my first day. Where is the middle school?"

I wanted to clear things up as soon as possible. Whenever I got nervous, the best thing to do was take charge of the situation. Mom didn't always like to take charge the way I did. She had a tendency to be a more back-seat type of person, while I was definitely a driver.

The front desk lady smiled at me as she took a thick stack of papers from Mom. "Welcome to Pelican Elementary School, Lucy! I'm Gabriella Garcia. You can call me Ms. Gabriella."

"Ms. Gabriella knows everything and she's the best!" One of the mailbox teachers handed her a steaming mug of coffee with the school logo on the side.

"Ms. Gabriella." I pressed my body against the counter to stop the small nervous tremors inside me. "I think there has been a terrible mistake. I'm in sixth grade. Where is the middle school?"

A girl with the same deep, dark eyes and round face as Ms. Gabriella stepped out of a small door marked Restroom behind the teacher's mailboxes. "Heron Junior High is for the seventh and eighth grade. Sixth grade goes to Pelican Elementary." Her clear voice carried across the small space between the counter and the mailboxes. I bet she was a very good singer. Each word seemed to be right on pitch.

"Junior high?" My fists clutched the counter and I kicked the thin rug with my tennis shoes. I felt like I had been tossed backward with a hard slam. I did not want to be in elementary school again.

"Sixth graders are the leaders at Pelican Elementary." Ms. Gabrielle filled a red folder with various sheets of colored paper, separating each paper into the two pockets. Her nails were jagged and her rough hands looked like they had been either gardening or cleaning a lot. She didn't have the fancy nails like Aunt Charlotte. She tucked a school calendar printed on red paper in the front of the folder.

"Lucy is a great leader!" Mom touched my shoulder. "I'm very proud of her."

I swallowed hard. Mom's praise always made me feel like I could really be someone. She didn't offer it often and when she did it always made me want to be the best version of me.

"The book fair is next week." Ms. Gabrielle handed me one of those newspaper type pamphlets with colored pictures of books on the front. "You can order with your class. Every class gets points for books. Thanks to some of our local businesses that sponsor our school, everyone gets to pick one free book."

"That's very nice." Mom plastered on a smile in that way she did when something wasn't really very nice. School book fairs were kind of a sore spot between Mom and me. In fifth grade, I had gotten my heart set on ordering an entire collection of nature journaling books with special colored pencils and brought it home to Mom. She had taken one look at it and I had received a thirty-minute lecture on how we couldn't afford to buy food and pay for the lights, so why did I think I would be getting a nature journal with colored pencils. Both of us were relieved when middle school didn't have the book fairs. But if I was going to have to be in elementary school again, then the book fairs were back. Ms. Gabrielle said we all got one free book. Maybe this time I really could pick out a book. I tucked the flyer into the front pocket of my backpack and zipped it.

My stomach grumbled and Ms. Gabrielle smiled at me. "Breakfast will be served in about ten minutes." She studied one of the papers Mom had given her and said to Mom. "Each student checks into their classroom and then everyone sits with their class for breakfast. It's free."

The school breakfast was always a giveaway that a school had kids with no money—or as the adults liked to call us, low-income children. In some schools, only a few kids in each class ate a breakfast meal and I was always one of them. At this school, all of us ate breakfast as a class which meant it was probably a Title I school, where most people got free or reduced-cost lunch and breakfast. I thought that was kind of odd, because there were so many nice big houses in Sea Rock Cove, and where did all the kids who lived in those big houses go to school? Aunt Charlotte had said there was only one school district, with three schools—one for each grade level.

Ms. Gabrielle finished telling Mom the bus number I would be on to go home just as kids poured through the open doors of the school in a loud clamor of voices and shouts. My stomach twisted. I didn't really think I could eat breakfast today. I just wanted to get to my class and find my desk and sit down. That soft, gooey feeling in my legs had increased, and I hoped I could make it down the hall to my class.

Mom turned to me. "I will see you after school, okay?"

"Sure." I nodded, hoping she could tell I didn't want her to give me a hug or a kiss. It was bad enough I had to be in elementary school again. I didn't want a goodbye kiss from my mom with kids all around me.

Mom read my mind, smiled at me and then hurried out the front door.

"Which way is my classroom?" I asked Ms. Gabrielle as three boys behind me jostled and shoved for a place at the counter. I guessed them to be about fourth grade, all physical and no brain smarts.

"I'll walk with you." The girl who had stepped out of the bathroom appeared beside me. "You're in the same class as me. I'm Sofia."

Sofia wore a flowered skirt with blue leggings, a red zip-up sweater and a pair of red sandals that showed off her painted toenails. She swept her glance over me and gave me what could only be called a disapproving look at my clothing choice of a baggy sweatshirt, too-big jeans and an old, beat-up pair of tennis shoes. I tried to dress so I didn't call any attention to myself on a first day, but maybe I had pushed it a little. I would never dress like Sofia, but I did have some nicer, light sweaters. I just figured because we were at the beach it must be a casual-dress type school. Sofia didn't seem to agree with me.

"How come you got to use the teachers' bathroom?" I asked Sofia as we made our way out of the office. Buses lined the circular driveway. Kids streamed off them and many called out to Sofia. She smiled and waved as we threaded our way down the hall swarming with kids of all ages.

"Ms. Gabrielle is my mom." Sofia shrugged. "I have to come to school early to watch my younger sister and brother while my mom works. There are some other kids who come to school early, too, who are teachers' kids. We go to the gymnasium and play games."

"Wow," I said. "That's a big job. Do you get paid?" I didn't think I would like to do a job like that, I didn't really like younger kids that much, but it was always good to know how to make some money in case Mom came up a little short.

Sofia eyed me. "No," she said. "I do it because it's the right thing for my family. They need me."

I was glad for the amount of noise in the hallway because I didn't want to tell Sofia I wasn't sure I would have been so noble about babysitting younger brothers and sisters every morning. Thankfully, Mom and Dad hadn't been able to have more kids so I never had to worry about what might have happened if I had siblings. It was hard enough sometimes just with Mom and me, when she needed me to do things.

As we walked down the hall, it was easy to see that the youngest grades were all placed at the front and the older grades were toward the end of the hallway. Colorful tags with teacher names and grade levels were plastered on the doors to each classroom. It didn't look like there were more than two classes for each grade level. Inside each classroom, it was the typical morning routine of kids coming in, leaving backpacks in the cubbies, sitting down at tables or in pods with morning work on their desk. Unlike a lot of schools that I had been to in Portland and Seattle, the teachers didn't seem so frazzled in this school. A few of them chatted with each other in the hallways, more than one held a steaming mug of coffee, and almost all of them smiled and called out good morning to Sofia. She seemed to prance through the school like it was her kingdom. So far, I wasn't sure I could fit into Sofia's Pelican Elementary School Kingdom, not if doing things like babysitting young siblings was a requirement, along with wearing pretty flowered skirts.

Finally, after what seemed like the longest walk, we reached the end of the hallway. Mr. Carson's Sixth Grade was printed on a colorful banner on the outside of the last door.

My heart pounded as I stepped into the room filled with

chatter, laughter, and an occasional high shriek of excitement. Mr. Carson was perched on his desk with three boys gathered around him. His long legs draped over the edge of the wooden desk, and he didn't seem to notice that a stack of papers had fallen to the red and orange, thinly carpeted floor. He wore faded blue jeans, work boots, and a flannel shirt. A fleece jacket hung over the back of a chair with a soft mesh back and a small red cushion. Behind him, a cork board filled a wall with motivational sayings and a picture of what was probably his wife and a child, about age six, in front of a waterfall, with tall evergreen trees in the background.

Mr. Carson's laugher filled the room as he rubbed what looked like an attempt at growing a beard and the boys around him jumped up and down. If nothing else, I had landed in a classroom with a teacher who didn't mind a little noise and seemed pretty relaxed as far as teachers go.

On the board, a digital screen said: Field Trip. Sea Rock. A picture of Sea Rock and birds flying in the air over the sea filled the entire white board where it was projected.

I couldn't believe it! I had the great fortune of landing on a field trip day, to—of all places—Sea Rock! I wanted to jump up and down and join in the classroom noise with a yee-haw of my own. Mom had promised me she would take me down at low tide, so we could see Sea Rock together. She said after the first time, I could probably go down on my own because the beach was only a couple of blocks from our house and she didn't see too much happening in the small town at this point in the season. I had hoped Mom and I would go to see Sea Rock on Sunday, but she had gotten involved with a little computer glitch which turned into all day, and she'd sent me to organize my room and pull some weeds around the cottages.

And now I had the great fortune to land on a field trip to

Sea Rock! I was going to see those sea stars Dad had always talked about and get started on my dream of becoming a marine biologist. All at once, like a particle dissolving, the fact that I had to attend an elementary school instead of a middle school didn't seem so bad.

"Lucy!" Mr. Carson called over the noise of the class jumping around the way every class does on a field trip morning. "I've been expecting you. Keep your bag with you. I'll show you around the classroom tomorrow after the field trip, okay?"

I grinned. Most of the time, teachers in the big schools didn't know my name, weren't expecting me, and didn't have time or patience to show a new girl where to keep her lunch or how the classroom procedures worked. They usually assigned me to some kid who didn't want to do it either and I was left to fend for myself after the first fifteen minutes.

Sofia turned from me and, with one of those high-pitched girl squeals, embraced a girl wearing capris and a navy sweatshirt. "Martina, my BFF!" she shrieked, adding to the general classroom clamor. "You're back!"

Martina's hair flowed down her back in a heavy, thick mass of curls. She flipped a hair band from her wrist and in one movement caught it up and tied it in a ball on her head.

Sofia said something in Spanish to Martina which I was obviously not supposed to hear. The two of them looked at me and then linked arms and walked over to a corner of the room with a big bean bag chair and a library of books spilling onto the floor. They sank down together in the beanbag chair. Martina pulled out a cell phone and showed something to Sofia. The two of them giggled and I felt the rock in my stomach. All the possible hope I'd been feeling seconds ago crashed in a crescendo in my chest. I peered around the room to see if anyone else was standing alone who I could talk to, but everyone was pretty much chattering to someone.

"Breakfast time, sixth graders! Be sure to take your bags and your science journals. We are not coming back to the classroom and will load the field trip bus from the cafeteria." Mr. Carson's voice boomed above the classroom noise.

In a flash, Sofia stood at the front of the line with Martina beside her, their arms looped. Martina held up her hand with a three-fingers up signal. Quiet. I sighed. In middle school, these silly little hand signals and line leaders didn't exist anymore.

The line of kids lowered their voices, but didn't completely stop talking, and Sofia and Martina led the class out the door and into the hallway. I stepped into the back of the line and followed. As we walked by each classroom, everyone walked with heads held up and the know-it-all stance that takes over a class when you are going on a field trip. I couldn't help but join in the hallway strut.

In the cafeteria, the lines quickly formed for hot and cold breakfasts. I placed a box of sugary cold cereal, milk and a banana on my tray. I skipped the eggs being ladled out with a plastic spatula onto the trays and veered off to find a place to sit in what looked like the class's section. This was always the hardest part of being new: eating in the cafeteria where everyone had already established their spots.

"Scoot over, Jordan." Mr. Carson not so gently nudged his hip against a heavyset boy. "This is Lucy and she needs a seat with our class." The boy grunted at me through a mouth of eggs and I sat down, half on the bench and half off. I quickly poured milk over my cereal and tried my best to swallow. I didn't dare look up. I knew what I would find. It was the same at every school meal on the first day. A couple of girls would be giggling and whispering while looking at me and then each other. A few girls would smile at me politely but make no motion toward becoming acquainted beyond a smile. And most of the boys would be too engrossed in their eating to notice me.

Thankfully, breakfast was over quickly, and I dumped my half-eaten soggy bowl of cereal, tucked my banana into my backpack and piled onto the bus with everyone else. I quickly saw that there were plenty of seats, even with the parent volunteers who stepped onto the bus in a small cluster, and I could spread out on a seat without being labeled a loner. I moved to the middle of the bus and plunked my backpack on the seat next to me so no one would sit down beside me. It was easiest this way, I told myself. For the twenty-minute ride to Sea Rock, I would not have to worry about making a friend. I could slink down into the deep green plastic seat and bury myself in my science notebook. Sofia and Martina moved past me without making eye contact. Something inside me ached. I never had a best friend. We moved too much, and I never had time to become anyone's BFF. But maybe at Sea Rock Cove it could be different. Maybe at Sea Rock Cove I could finally find a best friend. Someone to share all my secrets and adventures with, and sit in the corner on a beanbag chair while we poured over pictures on my cell phone about interesting marine life and science facts. A home was where you had a best friend and I wanted Sea Rock Cove to be home.

The bus started with a roar and everyone clapped as we pulled out of the school parking lot. My heart beat in time with the wheels as they moved faster and faster toward Sea Rock.

I was going to see Sea Rock. I was going to see Dad's sea stars!

4

TIDE POOLS

*A*s soon as the bus pulled into the public parking lot, I popped up in my seat and clutched the seat back. I recognized the parking lot from riding my bike on Saturday. We were in the cottage rental and hotel section of town, about three blocks from the cottages where Mom and I lived. Mr. Carson stood at the front of the bus and gave the hands-up quiet signal. It didn't take long for him to go over all the regular field trip rules and hand out small journals with pencils to each of us. "Record your observations," he said. "Everything you see and hear. It all goes in the journal."

I unzipped my backpack and tossed the journal inside. I already had my own scientific journal.

The class tumbled off the bus and fanned out into small partners and groups as we headed past a multiple-story hotel with a puffin sculpture in front. Sea Rock, a two-hundred-thirty-five-foot basalt Haystack Rock, towered ahead of us as we scrambled up and over a sand dune. The sea turned into cresting white waves and broke against the shore. The wind blasted across my face and I pulled up my hoodie, glad I had worn a sweatshirt and jeans for the first day of school. Sofia still wore her skirt, but a heavy green down jacket draped to the edges of her knees. Her eyes caught mine and she looped her arm through Martina's. The two of them snuggled together as they giggled and walked toward Sea Rock. I averted my eyes and pretended not to see them, but everyone else in the class had paired off into twos and threes too. It was hard not to admit that I was the odd girl out.

As we walked, Mr. Carson's voice carried over the wind, telling us Sea Rock had been created by a lava flow that once took place on the Oregon-Idaho border. The wide sandy beach seemed to stretch forever. Oregon Coast beaches weren't like beaches in California or on the East Coast. The water was always cold, too cold to swim or play in except on really hot days. Even then, swimmers didn't venture too far into the water because of the strong rip currents and cold waters. In the spring, there weren't too many people who sat on the sand with beach umbrellas, swimsuits and picnics. The wind and air were too cold for sunbathing until at least June, and even then it took a long time for the summer warmth to arrive. A couple of people, bundled up in fleece jackets and hats, were walking dogs along the shoreline, but mostly the beach was all ours as we headed toward Sea Rock, its form looming over the three-mile beach.

When we approached Sea Rock, I scanned the lower portion for sea stars. Mussels covered the basalt rock, but I didn't see any of the purple or orange ochre sea stars that matched Dad's tattoo. Were the sea stars still hidden under the tide? I knew there were three tide zones, and as the tide receded every twelve hours, each uncovered zone revealed different animals, including the mussels, barnacles and nudibranchs. I reached inside my sweatshirt and fingered my sea star necklace. The sea stars had to be here.

A bird swooping toward Sea Rock caught my eye. "Look at the eagle!" I ran to a beach telescope and swung it toward the bird soaring over the mammoth Sea Rock.

Flocks of seagulls, pigeon guillemots and common murres flapped their wings, cried loudly and flew off Sea Rock as the eagle soared in close and dove toward the peak.

"The eagle caught a bird!" A white-breasted, small bird dangled in the eagle's talons as it soared above our class. "A common murre!"

"Please don't move the telescope." A girl who looked to be in her early twenties, with a scarf wrapped around her neck and ear muffs on, strode toward me. "The scope is to see the puffin's nest." Strands of the girl's dark curly hair slipped from her tan cap which had "SEALS" stitched on the front. She wore a heavy, navy blue waterproof jacket, waterproof pants and black boots. A badge clipped to her heavy jacket identified her as "Sea Learning Specialist." She wore a separate name tag around her neck on a colorful purple, red and yellow lanyard with her name, Glory. Bunny stickers framed her name.

"Sorry." I stepped off the plastic two-stair footstool. In the time that I had been looking at the eagle, the class had moved into groups. One group clustered around the tide pools, another gathered around a folding table near a shiny blue truck with the same SEALS emblem as on the girl's hat plastered on the back of the truck. Each station had someone in a blue SEALS jacket and a parent volunteer who carried a pole with a picture of one of the nesting birds laminated on the front. The people in the blue jackets carried small yellow walkie-talkies and coordinated with each other. Did I miss the directions from Mr. Carson or was this something he had assigned earlier?

"Mr. Carson?" I strode up to him as he stood beside the folding table set up beside the SEALS truck. "I don't know my group." A trailer was hooked to the truck. Attached to the side were colorful painted signs that told visitors about the birds and the intertidal zone. Cars weren't allowed on the beach, but I guessed that SEALS was an exception.

"Whoops," Mr. Carson said. "Sorry, Lucy. I think I forgot to assign you one. How about you join this one?" He pointed to the table where seven kids clustered around a collection of laminated pictures of the different birds and an odd assortment of beaks, talons and eggs scattered across the table. I knew the names of most of the birds and could identify which beak, talon and egg went with which bird. Pretty much everyone had their journals and jotted down information. Sofia and Martina stood together sharing a notebook back and forth. Mr. Carson didn't say we could share notebooks, but maybe Sofia had special rules.

I grabbed my science notebook and pencil from my backpack. Mr. Carson didn't tell us exactly what to record in the journals. But I was good at taking observation notes.

I flipped to an empty journal page, about halfway through the notebook and recorded: Eagle. Common murre. I eyed the water level as it approached Sea Rock. It didn't look like low tide yet. I flipped to the front of my notebook where I had attached a tide table chart and checked the date. Low Tide: 10:33 a.m. We had left school at 8:00 a.m. It took us fifteen minutes to get to Sea Rock. It had to be only 9:00 a.m. at the latest, which would explain why I couldn't see Dad's sea stars yet; they hadn't been uncovered! I wrote *9:00 a.m.* and added a question mark beside my note. I liked to be precise and when I wasn't sure, I used question marks.

"Which egg belongs with which bird?" A tall, thin blonde girl wearing a blue SEALS jacket held out a tray full of large eggs. She didn't look very old, maybe in her early twenties. Her name tag said, Kyra, Volunteer Coordinator, SEALS. So she must be someone important, with coordinator after her name. Glory's name tag only said, Glory. Kyra had Corgi dog stickers around her name tag. If I had a SEALS name tag, mine would have sea stars.

"The spotted egg belongs to the common murre." I knew all my Sea Rock bird facts. The cottages had a big basket filled with colorful tourist travel brochures about the area. When we cleaned, I immediately fished all of the ones about sea life out of the basket and carted them off to my room to study. Sea Rock was a National Wildlife Refuge, which meant it was protected as a nesting habitat for sea birds, both the ones who migrated to Sea Rock every spring and the ones who lived there permanently.

"That's right," Kyra said. Her voice continued in a singsong tone, as if she had given this talk a hundred times. "The common murre use a common nest and mark their eggs so they can be identified."

"They only lay one egg," I said.

Sofia studied me and grabbed the notebook from Martina. She wrote very fast and pushed it back into Martina's hands. I didn't have to guess she was writing something about me. It didn't look like she was taking scientific notes on what I was saying. I tried not to let it show that I didn't like people writing notes about me when I was standing right there.

"Yes," Kyra said. She nodded to me and didn't break her lecture to the group. Her sharp blue eyes darted around the group as she talked, making sure each person was listening without saying a word. "The mother will leave after the chick hatches. It's the father who guides the chick down the rock and out to sea where it learns to swim and feed. Common murres are the best fathers in the bird kingdom."

"The eagle grabbed a common murre." My stomach tightened. Was he a father? Did he leave behind an egg? Was it too early to hatch? What would happen to the egg? Would the mother still leave? I jotted down notes fast in my notebook. Stay focused. I hummed to myself. Scientists did not get emotional. If an eagle snatched a common murre who was a father, it wasn't the same as a father who died in a fire and left behind a daughter.

Kyra's walkie-talkie crackled. She reached into her jacket and held the small yellow handpiece to her ear and said to everyone. "It's time for our very special treat. The welcome back puffin song!"

"We sing a song to the puffins?" Mom and I had lived in towns with German holiday markets, towns that fed oversized pumpkins to zoo animals on Halloween, and towns with summer festivals where people created makeshift boats. We'd never lived in a town that sang a song to birds.

"Yes." Sofia sidled up beside me with Martina by her side. "It's a tradition."

Was it also a tradition that Sofia and Martina always be together? It seemed to be.

"There's a puffin now!" Kyra pointed toward the sky as a small black bird with an orange beak fluttered off Sea Rock and quickly returned. The puffin was about the size of the common murre. Both birds flapped their wings in a small flutter, but the puffins had black bodies with orange bills and feet. The common murres had white bellies and no orange anywhere. In my notebook, I wrote: *Puffin. Right side of Sea Rock. 9:33 a.m.*

The other groups joined us from their stations with their parent volunteers and everyone clustered together.

"Everyone ready for the puffin song?" Kyra asked.

A chorus of voices erupted into cheers as the class formed into a circle. Kyra and two of the other SEALS instructors led us in singing a song to the tune of *The Muffin*

Man. Mr. Carson threw back his head and sang the loudest. *"Have you seen the puffin, man? The puffin, man? The puffin, man?"*

It didn't seem very scientific to sing to birds and I didn't sing. Glory leaned against the truck and studied the waves in the ocean. She didn't sing either, so I guessed it was okay if I wasn't singing, if one of the SEALS wasn't singing either.

When the song was over, Mr. Carson told us to change stations and follow the parent volunteers with the laminated signs. I trailed a tall woman with a puffin sign toward the left side of Sea Rock. A short, somewhat heavyset girl wearing a blue jacket waved us over to a small, six-foot rock covered with mussels, to the right of Sea Rock. "Stay on the sand. No trampling in the tide pools."

"Angelina!" Martina rushed out of our group and into the arms of the SEALS girl standing by the small rock. The two exchanged a long hug and it was hard not to miss the similarities in the shape of their eyes and facial structures. They looked to be either sisters or cousins.

As we gathered around, Angelina introduced herself, saying she was a senior at Heron High School. She was on a work-study program with SEALS. They needed an extra person to help with the field trip and she had been allowed to miss all her classes at Heron High School today. Angelina's SEALS name tag said Bilingual Interpreter and she had puffin stickers around her name.

"Starfish!" one of the students cried, and pointed toward an ochre sea star plastered against the side of the rock.

"Sea star!" My heart pounded. Dad's sea stars! Maybe Dad had gotten confused and they never were on the base of Sea Rock but on the smaller rocks, no bigger than six feet, that were clustered along the shoreline where tide pools formed at low tide.

"Yes," Angelina said to me, but loud enough so the whole group heard. "The correct name is sea star."

I pushed my way to the front until I was inches from the sea star. The body was smooth and an arm looked like it was close to falling off. "Something is wrong with the sea star." I peered closer. It should have had a white scaly pattern along the back, not something that looked like purple goop plastered against a rock.

"The sea star has the wasting syndrome." Angelina lowered her voice and the group pulled in close. Martina and Sofia stood next to Angelina as if all three of them were held together with the same center, a center that did not have a wasting syndrome.

I squatted closer so my nose was almost touching the sea star. "What's the wasting syndrome?"

"We aren't a hundred percent sure what's causing the syndrome, but there is a type of virus which has infected the sea stars. They don't grow to maturity, and they have been dying off for the last few years along the Pacific Coast," Angelina said. Her voice wasn't singsong like Kyra's, so I guessed she hadn't given as many field trip talks.

I pulled out my small notebook and wrote, *Sea Stars. Wasting Syndrome. Investigate.*

Sea Stars were a keystone species—that meant a lot of other species in their environment depended on them. The health of sea stars could tell you about the health of the whole intertidal zone.

"Is that why they aren't along the base of Sea Rock?" I asked without taking my eyes off the sea star.

"Correct," Angelina said. "The sea stars used to line the base of Sea Rock, but as the wasting syndrome moved through their species, they died off. We do see some at low tide and there is one here." Her voice brightened as if trying to convince us and herself that it was okay the ocean animals were sick and dying.

Dad had been right. Sea stars did once line the base of Sea Rock, but they were gone. I stood up and stepped away from the group, not really wanting to see any more of the sea stars wasting. Something inside me felt empty and hollow. I fingered my necklace. Dad was gone and his sea stars were gone. Even though I knew it wasn't the same, it still felt like something had hit me in the stomach in a big whoosh.

A tall man walked with his yellow Lab along the edges of the water. The Oregon Coast allowed dogs to be off-leash and under voice control. In the hour or so we had been at Sea Rock, I had seen a few people walking with dogs off-leash. The dogs chased balls and ran freely, sniffing the driftwood high above the tide line.

The man walked next to the shore but kept his dog close by his side on a leash. He walked at a good clip and as he got closer, I recognized him as the man from the porch with his painting on an easel. His dog squatted to poop, and the man slipped a blue plastic dog poop bag out of his jacket. But before he could scoop, the wind caught the bag and it tumbled over the sand toward me. Trash on the beach was very bad for the birds, who sometimes thought it was food. I had watched a whole documentary about birds with plastics inside their stomachs because they had eaten the shiny food, and then they tried to regurgitate it to feed to their young. I didn't want that to happen to any of the birds of Sea Rock.

I ran toward the bag, and as it tumbled like a tumbleweed in the desert breeze, I leaned over and scooped it up. The man approached and I handed him the bag. He was tall and towered over me, his thick white hair blew in the wind. He wore black jeans, a heavy black sweatshirt and tall boots like people wore to fish in rivers or stand in oceans.

"Thank you," he said, as he took the bag from me, his voice deep and gruff. It wasn't the kind of thank you people said when they wanted you to stay and talk to them. It was the kind of thank you that said hurry up and leave me alone.

Something inside me shivered. I didn't want to stay and talk to him and his dog like I did with Thomas and Luna.

"Lucy!" I turned around at the sound of Sofia's voice. She motioned me to her in quick hurried motions.

I ran back to the group. They were listening to Angelina explain about the mussels on the rock and how there were more of them because the sea stars weren't there to eat them. My heart pounded inside my sweatshirt in what sounded like a loud *thump thump*.

Sofia grabbed my arm as I reached her. "You talked to him?" she said, her words thick and choked.

"I gave him his poop bag," I said. "It got too far away in the wind and he couldn't catch it." I didn't think a thank you counted as talking to someone.

"He's scary." Sofia widened her eyes and Martina nodded in agreement.

"Something happened to him. No one talks about it," Martina said, her voice lowered as if she was telling me a secret.

"Everyone stays away," Sofia said in the same lowered voice, as if she and Martina were one voice.

Angelina's walkie-talkie crackled and she announced it was time for us to change stations. She stepped over to Martina and said something in Spanish, her voice filled with warmth. The two embraced, then Martina looped arms with Sofia and the two walked toward the tide pools, following our adult volunteer.

A dog barked and I looked down the beach toward the sound. The man's yellow Lab jotted down the beach, chasing a ball. The man's shoulders slumped forward, and he trailed after him as if he carried a lot of sadness. Just like Mom and I when we found out Dad died in the fire. I knew that, sometimes, what looked to be fierce and scary was really the protection people wrapped around themselves when they had something happen which hurt. I used the scary-mean self-protection when the counselors wanted to talk to me after Dad died. I wouldn't answer any of their helpful talk-about-it questions. Sometimes I hid in the bathroom and said I was sick so I didn't have to go to school counseling hour.

Who was this man? What had happened to him? Was his scary gruffness his protection from something bad? Mom and I had known people who others thought were scary or bad, but once you got to know them you found out they weren't so scary. I huddled into my sweatshirt as a gust of wind blasted around me. Sea Rock loomed over me, the tide pushing out, the base of Sea Rock covered in mussels, not sea stars.

I turned back to look at the melting purple sea star. Dad's sea stars were sick and dissolving in front of my eyes.

OUR NEXT SEA Rock field trip station was the tide pools in front of Sea Rock. The tide had receded enough to reveal small pools of water nestled among small rocks, not bigger than six feet across and one foot high, stepping-stone type rocks.

"Please stay on the sand." Glory unzipped her blue SEALS coat as the sun moved from behind a cloud and shone onto the tide pools. "No trampling in the tide pools."

Small hermit crabs burrowed into the sand. Giant green anemones opened their emerald-green tentacles. The animals were about twelve inches in diameter. Some were attached to the rocks. Out of the water their discs were closed. I noted in my journal the size and shape of the anemones by drawing wide circles.

I didn't see any sea stars in the tide pools.

I walked around the tide pools, making sure to stay on the sand, until I reached the front of Sea Rock. Barnacles and mussels two and three feet deep covered the lower portion of the rock. The area below the rock was filled with loose rock and a chain hung from two small posts. A small metal sign hung from the middle of the chain. No Climbing.

I grinned. This must have been where Dad and Thomas tried to climb Sea Rock.

No sea stars at the base of Sea Rock, I recorded in my journal.

Another sign stuck out of the sand: Nesting birds. I couldn't see any nesting birds. Why would a bird nest at the bottom of the rock? I craned my neck and peered upward. Grass covered the right side where the puffins had made their burrows and shared the space with the common murres. The puffins knew to make their nests up high and away from human disturbance.

The tide surged and water lapped at my feet and easily moved into my thin-soled tennis shoes. The next time we went to the thrift store, I needed to find tall waterproof boots like Glory's.

I turned my face to the ocean. The baby blues in the sky and the deep sapphire blue in the ocean combined to such a blur, I felt I could taste the color. I stuck my tongue out and the cold spring air blew across it. Shivering, I pulled my hood up over my head again. I needed a warmer jacket.

I liked the tide pools because we could wander around by ourselves. Glory seemed to have a hands-off approach and I liked it. Sofia and Martina stood at the other end of the tide pools, far away from me. But just as I was making more notes,

Glory's walkie-talkie crackled and it was time to switch stations. Our parent volunteer hustled us into a group and led us toward the grassy dunes which faced the ocean.

At the dunes, a girl who looked to be about mid-twenties, with dark hair pulled into braids, met us. She wore black pants, black boots and a black top. Her blue SEALS jacket hung open and her pockets sagged with what looked like trash. Her SEALS name tag said Autumn, with small paint-brush stickers around it. Just like Kyra, she also had a second tag attached to her coat that said "Sea Learning Specialist Director."

One of the boys snickered at her name as she introduced herself. She stared at him with what could only be described as a stare which said, *Never cross me. Ever.* I figured as director she must know how to set people in their place. I made a note to learn that stare. It could be very useful.

A row of white one-gallon paint buckets stood behind her.

"Find a friend or two and grab a bucket," she told us, in what sounded like a voice muffled by a stuffed-up nose. Her walkie-talkie crackled more than any of the others. The voices of the other SEALS blended together as they came across on Autumn's walkie-talkie. She reached over and turned it down. "Sorry," she said. "Sometimes they forget to turn off their walkie-talkies when they are giving their talks." On her left hand, she wore what looked like a small diamond wedding or engagement ring.

I picked up one of the paint buckets. Each bucket had a pair of gloves tucked inside and I pulled mine on.

"We're going to pick up beach trash," Autumn said.

"What trash?" Martina swung her bucket back and forth in time with Sofia who was doing the same motion.

I agreed with Martina. The beach seemed pretty clean to me. Large pieces of driftwood lay against the dunes and formed small sitting areas where spring beachgoers had braved the cold evenings and built bonfires; pieces of burnt wood were tucked in among the deep sand.

Autumn kneeled and scooped up tiny pieces of what looked like broken plastic. She motioned for all of us to step closer. "Microplastics." She dropped the small purple, black and grey pieces into the bucket by her feet. "You can find microplastics in the tide lines. Look closely along the seaweed."

Why did we need such big buckets if this was our beach trash? It was going to take a long time to fill the buckets with these little pieces. The look on Sofia's face said she was thinking the same thing as me. I chewed back a laugh.

"Be sure to wear the gloves in your buckets, and spread out in a straight line." Autumn pointed to the empty lifeguard stand. The lifeguards arrived on Memorial Day weekend and stayed until Labor Day. "Stop at that point, and ..." She paused and searched the other way down the beach. "Stop at the farthest dune before the hotel on the end."

Martina and Sofia joined arms and walked toward the hotel, their buckets still swinging in time and their heads pressed together. It looked like both of them were out for a beach stroll and not a pick-up-beach-trash job. Autumn didn't say we were getting graded on how much trash we picked up, and Mr. Carson had been sitting in the SEALS truck with a cup of coffee since we looked at the wasting sea star.

I took a couple of steps toward the lifeguard stand. It didn't take long to see the microplastics. The small pieces seemed to pop out of the sand everywhere. I couldn't believe there could be so many, or that I hadn't noticed them as we walked along the beach. I was a scientist and noticed everything. How had I missed the microplastics?

Autumn stepped up beside me. "Eight million tons of

plastic enters the ocean every year." She shook her head and her braids bobbed alongside her shoulders. "People don't think about what they're doing. The oceans can't continue to be trash cans. The pollution is killing off species every day."

"The sea stars too." I scooped up three pieces of blue plastic and dumped them in my bin. Small, colorful pieces littered the entire tide line as far as I could see. It wasn't the plastic sand pails and shovels that little kids brought to the beach and sometimes left lying beside half-built sandcastles which caused the microplastics. It was something much bigger. Something we were doing that sent the plastics to the sea and caused them to wash ashore broken into pieces in the tide lines. And it was hurting the ocean ecosystem.

"The sea stars are sad." Autumn's eyes clouded. She blinked hard. "They used to line the lower edges of Sea Rock, two and three deep, purple and orange as far as the eye could see. But that's all gone now."

"My Dad told me about them," I said. "He had a sea star tattoo on his upper left arm because he loved them so much. I have a sea star necklace he gave me." I reached into my shirt and pulled out the necklace to show Autumn. "There has to be a way to help them."

Autumn looked over my head toward the sea. She didn't say anything. If she was director of the SEALS, I thought she must be pretty smart and know a lot about the ocean. Mr. Carson seemed like a nice teacher, but I wasn't sure how much he knew about the ocean, especially because he seemed more interested in his coffee and the warm truck than our field trip.

"Do you have a business card?" I said in my best grown-up voice. "In case I have some questions."

Autumn grinned at me. Her smile brightened her round

face and she reached into her jacket's inner pocket and pulled out a small card. "Here you go."

I took the card. The SEALS emblem and her name were printed across the front. I tucked the card inside my journal. "Thank you," I said, in a voice that was one that grown-ups used that said we'll be talking more, a lot more. One day I wanted to come out to Sea Rock and instead of recording in my journal there were no sea stars, I would write, "Hundreds of sea stars seen along the base of Sea Rock."

5

THE WRONG PUFFIN

*W*e barely got back to school before it was time to pack up and go home. I didn't have much to pack up because I hadn't gotten books or assignments yet. Mr. Carson said not to worry, and he would set me up with everything I needed tomorrow. We all lined up according to our bus number and Mr. Carson walked along the line, checking his clipboard and making sure we were on the right bus. Sofia stood at the back of the line for the kids who were going to the library to get picked up by their parents. Martina stood next to me in the bus line, so I knew she also rode the Sea Rock Cove bus home. It was the first time I had seen Sofia and Martina apart all day.

Mr. Carson walked us out to the circular driveway, checking his clipboard as kids got onto the buses. On the bus, kids of all ages filled the seats. I sat down in the only open spot, next to what looked to be a first or second grader. The bus ride from Pelican Shores to Sea Rock Cove took fifteen minutes, most of it on the same highway Mom and I had traveled on when we arrived on Saturday. The first grader spent most of the ride telling me about the new pet hamster in their classroom and how they were going to get to take it home over the summer break. I hoped it didn't die like the hamster I took home one year in my third-grade class. When we arrived in Sea Rock Cove, the bus stopped near a small park in the north end, with picnic tables and a restroom, and a ton of kids got off. I peered out the window at the small and midsized cottage homes along gravel roads. None of them had vacation rental signs.

The school bus lumbered down Main Street, past the shops and the crooked art gallery. The man wasn't sitting on the deck, but the door was open and his dog lay in the doorway. The bus stopped in the middle of the hotel area. I was the only kid to get off there. The bus was still half full and as it drove away, Martina pressed her face against a back window. She didn't acknowledge me. I took a deep breath. The first day of school was over.

The cottage parking lot had three cars; a black Subaru was parked on one side of a white Honda CR-V with California plates, and a silver BMW with Washington plates was on other side.

"Lucy!" Mom stood in front of the open door to the laundry room off our back entrance. Colorful sheets and towels lay on the floor in a heap. "I need your help making up some cottages. The reservation calendar isn't updated, and I had no idea we had guests arriving. There's also some kind of book festival this weekend and the phone has been ringing off the hook looking for last-minute cancelations."

One of Mom's jobs had been a hotel cleaning attendant. On days I didn't have school, she took me with her. I liked refilling the shampoo and soap containers in the shower, but I couldn't ever tuck in the sheets tight enough, so she usually made the beds. We made it work and got the job done. Now we needed to make it work at Sea Rock Cove.

"Cottage five needs to have extra towels." Mom consulted a clipboard. "Take the cleaning caddy, too, in case you need to dust anything." She peered out the window. "I think another couple just arrived." She bit her lower lip.

"No problem." I tossed a stack of fluffy yellow towels into a laundry basket, picked up the cleaning caddy filled with an odd assortment of rags and cleaning bottles, and headed toward cottage five. A black and white Golden Doodle bounded out of the BMW and lurched toward a white bunny huddled by the front walkway. Another bunny scurried toward the recycling bins behind cottage three. The woman yanked hard on the leash and muttered something about rabbits not being a good fit around dogs. We were going to have to do something about the bunnies. I could already see the bad reviews posted on the travel websites.

I turned the doorknob of cottage five and stepped into a small room decorated in blues, whites and yellows. A yellow plush chair faced a cozy fireplace. I ran my fingers along the mantel and beside a conch shell. A layer of dust coated everything.

I wiped down the two-person table, noting the scratches in the left corner. Mom always liked to know about these things so she could document the damage had been there already, before guests arrived. Once everything had been wiped down, I opened the kitchen cabinet under the sink and pulled out a pretty white vase. I grabbed a pair of scissors from the top drawer and stepped outside the cottage to the blooming pink rhododendron. Guests always liked flowers.

I moved into the small bedroom off the living room. It was barely big enough for me to turn around in with the bed. A small bathroom was attached to the room. I placed the extra towels inside a cabinet under the sink.

When I finished, the woman with the dog stood in the doorway. "Can I bring my stuff in?"

"Everything is ready," I said in my best grown-up voice. It was important Mom and I work as a team and make the guests happy. Mom's job at the cottages gave us our ticket to staying in Sea Rock Cove and I needed to be here to find out more about the sea stars and hear stories about Dad from Thomas and other people who might have known him. Sea Rock Cove was going to be my home too.

The woman dropped a duffle bag onto the floor and settled into the plush yellow chair. Her dog lay beside her.

"The dog yard is to the side," I said. "There are waste bags attached to the pole." I liked that we were a pet-friendly place, especially on the Oregon Coast where dogs could be off-leash and under voice control.

I gathered my cleaning supplies and slipped out the cottage. A black rabbit darted to the left of me as I walked to our back door.

"Everything is good," I said to Mom as I dropped the cleaning caddy and empty laundry basket. "But the bunnies are a problem for the dogs."

Mom frowned. "I need to find out more about the bunnies. I'm not sure where they are coming from or who owns them." Mom touched my shoulder. "I was so busy, I didn't even get to ask you how school was today."

"Okay." I shrugged. "We went on a field trip to see Sea Rock. Dad's sea stars aren't there anymore. They have a wasting syndrome. Can I go to the library for a while?" It had been closed on Saturday morning when I tried to go after talking to Aunt Charlotte. The sign said it was only open from

1:00 p.m. to 5:00 p.m. every day. That didn't seem like a lot of hours to me.

"Of course," Mom said. "Let me know if you need help with getting a card."

I ducked my head and smiled. Mom knew all about my colorful collection of library cards. I always got a library card from every town we lived in. I had a small stack of them tucked away in a zipped pouch I'd found at a Goodwill. I arranged them by color, with all the darker color cards first and the lighter colors in the back.

I hopped on the bike and it didn't take long to pedal downhill to town. As I pedaled by the art gallery, the yellow Lab raised his head and looked at me. He wagged his tail but I kept pedaling. I wasn't going to stop to visit with that dog, not until I found out a little bit more about the man who no one wanted to talk to.

The library was next to the post office. Across the street, Thomas played his guitar for a group of diners. It seemed cold to eat outside to me, but the guests wore fleece jackets and didn't seem to mind. Luna lay by his side at his open guitar case and dollar bills filled the case. I waved, but he didn't see me.

I parked my bike in one of the spaces in the bike rack. The double doors to the library opened to a good-sized room. A local newspaper was spread across a wooden table in front of a stone fireplace. Adult mysteries and fiction books filled bookcases all around the room. A dark-haired woman worked behind a desk.

"Can I help you?"

"I need to do some research online." I cleared my throat. "For school." For some reason it always made me feel better to tell the librarians my research was for school. It made me sound more legitimate and not like one of those kids who went to libraries to play computer games.

The librarian guided me to a computer on a small desk. She logged into the computer and opened the browser. "It's all yours. The printer is behind you. We don't charge for printed pages."

I knew just how to research. I pulled up the database for scientific journals and typed in my key words. What was this sea star wasting syndrome? How long had it been going on? What had been done about it?

I read through the article abstracts and tagged a couple from University of Southern California. The sea star wasting syndrome (SSWS) had first been found in sea stars along the Washington coast in June 2013.

Much of the sea star population along the Pacific coast had died off the following summer, in 2014, and had not returned. Some thought it was environmental and wanted to blame it on the disaster at the Fukushima nuclear facility in Japan in 2011, others thought it was warming oceans, but nothing linked it for sure to either. That was the problem. It seemed that no one could figure out why the sea stars had died. The wasting occurred quickly, just as Angelina had told us. The lesions appeared and there was a decay of tissues immediately after, often within hours. At the rate we were going, the sea stars could become extinct. There weren't a lot of animals that ate sea stars besides the gulls and sea otters, and the Oregon Coast didn't have many sea otters. But the more important thing was that the sea stars were needed to feed on the mussels, which otherwise would take over the rocks, not leaving room for other animals. The sea stars were a keystone species for the intertidal zone, and without them, the whole intertidal zone was in danger of tipping over.

The librarian tapped me on the shoulder. "I'm sorry to

interrupt you, but we are closing soon. Can I help you with anything?"

"No, thank you." I stood and gathered my things. I guess small-town libraries didn't need to stay open at night like the ones in the city. In cities, people who didn't have homes went to the libraries when it got cold. Cities also had warming shelters. I saw the alerts on Mom's phone sometimes in severe cold winter weather. Where did Thomas and Luna go when it got cold if they didn't have a house?

I unhooked my bike and rode across the street. Thomas had stopped playing his guitar and was sorting his dollar bills.

"Lucy Lavender," he said, and smiled at me.

I kneeled and gave Luna my hand. She sniffed and then bowed her head. Softly, I scratched her soft brown and black fur.

"How are you?" I asked Thomas.

"Couldn't be better." He pointed to his stack of folded bills. "I'm going to have a nice dinner tonight and Luna is going to get a nice treat, too. How was your day?"

"We went on a field trip to Sea Rock. The sea stars are gone."

Thomas peered at me. "Gone? I've seen a few when Luna and I spend the night out there. Shhh ..." He turned around and looked over his shoulder. "You're not supposed to overnight camp on the city beaches, but most of the time we escape notice. We pack up our things early in the morning and take a walk with the other beach walkers and dogs. We blend right in." He chuckled.

I wanted to ask Thomas about the man with the yellow Lab at the art gallery, but Thomas picked up his guitar, pocketed all the dollar bills and slipped the guitar inside the case. He tipped his tall top hat at me. "You have a good night. It's a good day today. Soak it up."

Luna trailed along beside him as they headed down the street and toward a steak and seafood restaurant.

I cruised up the hill on my bike and around the backside of the art gallery. There were a lot of two- and three-story homes that faced the ocean. All of them had the same brown shingles that the smaller ones did. Most of them were empty and a few had the vacation rental signs attached. I guessed there weren't any kids who lived in these houses because the bus had only dropped me off at my stop. I turned left into a small area of boutique hotels, a surf shop, and one very tall hotel that went on for blocks.

Glory loped out of the surf shop. She nodded her head at me and ambled over. She wore a long, baggy, brown overcoat over brown slacks and boots, but no scarf or earmuffs. "I remember you." She snapped her fingers. "You're the one who didn't sing the puffin song."

"You didn't sing either." I crossed my arms in front of my chest.

"No." She shrugged. "It's not really my thing."

"That puffin isn't the right puffin." I nodded toward a five-foot painted wood statue standing in front of the hotel. "That is an Atlantic puffin. The tufted puffins at Sea Rock have a black body with a white head. The tufts of feathers are common in the mating season."

She studied me. "You're smart. I could tell at the tide pools. You were more interested than everyone else."

"How can I get a job at Sea Rock? I need to study the sea stars and find out more about their wasting syndrome." Angelina said she had a work-study program with SEALS; maybe they had one for me too. I could make some money for Mom and me, and study the sea stars while writing a big report for the researchers.

Glory studied me for a minute and then said. "Junior

volunteer. They're kids under eighteen who help us out. You need to talk to Autumn. She's in charge of the SEALS."

Talking to Autumn was easy. I had her card. "Why are you called SEALS?"

Glory scrunched up her nose. "Sea Learning Specialists." She shook her head. "It's our official name. But it's stuffy, and doesn't really suit any of us who work on the beach. So we came up with SEALS and everyone loved it."

"SEALS." I grinned. I could be a junior SEALS. I could give talks like Angelina and Kyra, and tell people not to trample on the tide pools like Glory. And, I could collect data. The first step in all good science projects was data collection.

Glory eyed the sky. "I gotta go. Tide's going to be going out soon and I want to get my board."

"Isn't it cold in the water?" I shivered. I couldn't imagine getting into the water with the air so cold.

"We wear wetsuits," Glory said and smiled at me. "It's the only way to surf on the Oregon Coast. You should come out and try it some time."

"Maybe." I couldn't stop grinning. I'd love to surf with Glory. I'd love to do anything with Glory!

Thomas was right. It was a good day today and I was going to soak it up.

6

RULES OF SEA ROCK

On Saturday, I headed down the beach in a quick gallop toward Sea Rock. It had been easy to call Autumn, using the number on her business card, and add my name to the junior SEALS volunteers. Autumn talked to Mom for a few minutes and said I could fill out all the paperwork on my first shift on Saturday. Autumn asked if I could start on Friday afternoon for a few hours to get used to things, but Mom told her I was needed to help check in guests at the cottages. It was a busy weekend with the literary festival, and she needed all the help she could get. Mom said I could go on Saturday morning to Sea Rock because everyone would be settled and headed out to get coffee at the nearby coffee shop before taking beach walks and heading to the festival.

Small, blue, translucent cellophane items lay all over the beach and there was a fishy smell in the air. I picked up one of the slippery pieces. Did a cargo ship overturn and the tide wash in trash? We needed a big clean-up of all these things! What if they were what was endangering the sea stars? I pulled out my science journal from my backpack and made some notes, looking at the size, texture and shape.

The blue SEALS truck and trailer were parked in the usual place in front of the tide pools. Glory lifted the tailgate and hoisted two sandwich board signs. She leaned one against the truck. She carried the other and placed it in front of Sea Rock. *No collecting. No trampling. No climbing.*

A drone soared high in the air above my head.

Suddenly, Glory dropped the sign. She charged down the beach to a couple of boys with a drone remote. Glory waved her hands, pointed at Sea Rock and shook her head.

The boys brought their drone to the sand and moved further down the beach, away from us.

Glory strode back and picked up the sign. "Constant problem," she muttered. "We're trying to get the drones banned from the beach. They aren't allowed anywhere near Sea Rock because the birds are nesting."

"What are the blue pieces of trash all over the beach?" I asked.

"Trash?" Glory frowned.

"The smelly things that look like small pieces of plastic?"

Glory laughed. "Velella velella. They wash in every spring. Eventually they'll dry out and wash away."

A cocker spaniel sniffed along the tide line as his owner walked behind carrying a ball and long throw stick. "Do dogs eat the velella velella? Are they harmful?"

"I don't think so." Glory nodded in the direction of the dog trotting toward us. "The dog can't be off leash around the tide pools. This is a protected marine garden." We watched for a few minutes as the owner clipped the leash back onto the dog, waved at us as they walked by the tide pools and then unclipped the dog further down the beach.

Glory smiled. "She's local. She knows the rules."

A small crowd gathered at the tide pools. "The spring beach weekends have started," Glory said. "It's going to be extra crowded today because of the literary festival. Angelina is going to come down and help out, and she's bringing Martina because we need extra people."

I danced a little jig and rubbed my hands together. I couldn't wait to start my volunteer job as a junior SEALS, even if I wasn't very excited to see Martina on Saturday. She and Sofia hadn't warmed up to me at school at all, even though we had been assigned to sit in the same table pod together. A couple of times I caught Mr. Carson watching us, but I never let on that the two of them really didn't work with me on the math problems, and I was left on my own to finish the reading journal.

I hoped SEALS junior volunteering was very different from school. I hadn't had much luck making friends the first week of school. It seemed everyone knew each other and already had their friendships formed. It was okay, I told myself. But now that I was a junior SEALS, maybe there would be other kids here to meet. Kids like me who were interested in the ocean. Friends didn't have to be your same age, so maybe Glory and I could be friends.

Glory and I strolled to the trailer and Glory opened the side doors. Everything was neatly organized. Blue jackets were stored in two plastic bins according to size. Smaller containers held the plastic sea stars and bird parts which I'd seen set up on the table during our field trip. There was a basket for binoculars in small brown cases.

Glory reached into a small basket attached to the door and dug around a bunch of tags. She pulled out one. "Here's yours."

Lucy, Junior Volunteer

I clipped the name tag to my shirt and made a note to get

sea star stickers at the Dollar Store where Mom shopped. Voices behind me chattered and I turned around to see Angelina with Martina and another girl that I didn't recognize. She was the same height as Martina, about four foot eleven, and wore a light blue wind jacket, jeans with embroidered flowers on the left pant leg, tall wading boots like Glory, and her blonde hair was pulled into a ponytail that stuck out of her SEALS cap. Her face was very darkly tanned, which I thought was odd because no one was getting a tan at this time of the year on the Oregon beaches. I shuffled my feet in the sand. But I had been right. There were going to be other junior volunteers!

Angelina smiled at me and said, "Isabella, I'd like you to meet our newest junior volunteer. This is Lucy."

Isabella eyed me. She wasn't as chummy with Martina as Sofia was, but the two of them still seemed to be very friendly and know each other well.

"Do you go to Pelican Elementary School, too?" I asked, trying to be polite. There were two sixth grade classes at the school, so maybe Isabella was in the other class. I didn't recognize her, but she could have been absent this week and that explained her tan.

"No." Isabella shook her head. "I live in Seattle. We have a house here," she waved her arm toward the north end of the beach. "We come out sometimes on weekends and during the summer."

"She just got back from Hawaii on her spring break," Martina said. "Lucky girl was swimming with the turtles on the Big Island."

That explained the tan. Isabella's family must have money. I didn't know anyone who had ever been to Hawaii. Well, I guessed Aunt Charlotte had probably been to Hawaii, she seemed like she probably traveled a lot of places, but most of the people Mom and I knew barely had enough money to eat out on special occasions.

But if Isabella was only here on weekends, why did she volunteer? I would think if she only came out on weekends, she would want to hang out like the tourists and not do things like volunteer. "How come you volunteer with SEALS if you are only here sometimes?" I blurted.

"I want to be a veterinarian," Isabella said, she didn't look at me. "It's good experience to volunteer."

I knew she was lying. Most twelve-year-olds didn't like to volunteer. I was doing it because I had a bigger purpose—to save Dad's sea stars. Martina had to be here because Angelina was her older cousin and they needed an extra hand on the beach today. I wasn't fooled. Isabella had to be here for another reason. Had she gotten in trouble somehow and now had to do one of those volunteer community service things? Or did her parents just want her out of their way so they could relax at their beach house?

Sofia said her mom, Ms. Gabriella at the school office, worked for a family who came from Portland over the weekend. She cleaned their house and got it ready for them on Friday after school while Sofia took care of her sisters and brothers. After the weekend was over, she went back and cleaned up the people's house again. She also ran errands for them if they needed a big grocery store run from the superstore and didn't want to go themselves. Sofia took care of her siblings while her mom ran these errands and cleaned houses for other families. Most of the people Mom and I knew did a couple jobs, because you just had to in order to make rent. I bet Isabella's parents didn't work two jobs.

"Time to work, SEALS." Glory hoisted a hand-painted picture of two puffins out of the side compartment of the trailer. "Lucy, can you help me get these on the side of the truck? There are eight of them and each slides into the racks on the doors of the trailer. There's a number on the back of each panel."

Martina and Angelina picked up a handful of laminated signs stuck to small thin poles. They carried them toward the tide pools while Isabella walked along beside them, chatting to Martina. Isabella didn't help as Martina and Angelina stuck the signs in the sand around the tide pools. I picked up a panel from a rack inside the truck. It was heavy and took some muscle to get it into the slot. But I could do it. I wanted to show Glory I was very capable of doing what was asked of me, unlike Isabella.

"Got it?" Glory asked as I slid the board into place.

"Where's the next one?" I asked and flexed my arm into a muscle.

Glory pointed to the row of panels inside the trailer and I hefted the next one out. I focused on hanging each panel straight. As I was finishing the last one, a man and a woman tapped me on the shoulder.

"Can you tell us how Sea Rock got to be here? We're from Connecticut. The Oregon Coast is so different from the East Coast."

"A lava flow came from the Columbia Basin about fifteen to sixteen million years ago," I replied. I had memorized the colorful panels as I hung them. In the one about Sea Rock, sea stars lined the base just like Dad had said. In the left-hand corner of each panel, there was a small artist signature that said Max There was a last name too, but I couldn't make it out. It looked like it started with an L, or maybe an H. Could the artist who made the signs for the truck be the same man I had seen on the porch with his dog? The panels looked like the paintings I saw on the front porch and in the window of his gallery.

"Thanks, Lucy," Glory said as the tourists moved away. "You'll find out that people pretty much ask the same questions. It's not hard once you get the hang of it."

She shivered as a blast of wind whipped around the truck. "Grab one of the heavy SEALS jackets from the bin. The small ones are on top. It gets cold out here."

I opened the door and pulled out a zip-up blue jacket with a hood from the bin. The SEALS emblem was printed on the left-hand side, and across the back of the jacket it said SEALS at Sea Rock. Even though I selected a small one, the arms were huge. I swam inside the sleeves.

"Here," Glory said, and laughed. "Let me help you."

She rolled up the sleeves and shook her head. "It'll have to do. How about you stand by the tide pools with Isabella?"

Standing by Isabella wasn't really where I wanted to be. I would have preferred to hang out with Glory, but it was better than standing with Martina and Angelina, who were at the base of Sea Rock by the roped-off portion. A group of women clustered around Martina who pointed upward to the nesting birds on Sea Rock. Angelina stood nearby talking to a couple with a small toddler.

I trotted off to the tide pools where Isabella stood like a statue, not even looking while a little boy leaned into the tide pools and touched a giant green sea anemone's tentacles that were opening and closing.

"Excuse me," I said in my best grown-up voice. "Please don't touch the animals in the tide pools."

"We're sorry," a petite woman pulled the boy away from the anemone. "My son brought a container to collect a few things."

"No collecting." I pointed to the sandwich board sign.

The boy stepped into the tide pools with a hard *thunk*. Water splashed onto the sand.

"Please," I said in my best patient voice. "We don't want to trample on the animals living in the tide pools. Stay on the sand." Again, I pointed to one of the signs Martina and Angelina had stuck in the sand next to the tide pools.

"Okay." The woman yanked her son out of the tide pools. "We'll try to follow the rules."

Isabella pulled out a fancy cell phone and scrolled. Her jacket sleeve moved and a fancy black wrist band showed the time and a text. I hadn't seen anyone at Pelican Elementary who had a matching cell phone and wristband. She ignored me as her cell phone dinged and she texted something back. I knew we weren't supposed to have our cell phones. Autumn told Mom I couldn't bring anything with me, especially my cell phone. Mom asked if it was okay if I had my science journal and Autumn said I could have that if I only wrote in it when I wasn't busy talking to guests.

If Isabella was interested in volunteering, then why wasn't she helping out? And why didn't Glory say something to her? Didn't she have to follow the SEALS junior volunteer rules too?

Suddenly, loud bird cries erupted from the rock. Birds dove off in a feverish flurry.

"What's happening?" the woman asked.

"An eagle." I pointed toward the bird swooping over Sea Rock.

Isabella slipped her phone into her jacket and peered upward.

The eagle dove and then swept above us toward the trees on the hillside. I was pretty sure a small bird, most likely a common murre, hung from the talons. The woman gasped.

She picked up her son and moved him away from the tide pools and toward the hotel buildings on the bluff facing Sea Rock.

"It's not a zoo out here," Glory said, and adjusted her earmuffs as she stepped up beside us. "It's nature. People don't always like seeing the eagles get a bird, but it's all part of the ecosystem."

Isabella kept her cell phone in her pocket and told Glory how she talked to the woman all about the tide pools. I bit the inside of my mouth so hard I tasted blood. Isabella hadn't talked about the tide pools. I had. Why was Isabella telling Glory it was her?

The wind blew hard and I shivered. I pulled up my hood. The jackets were waterproof but not warm.

"You can hop in the truck if you get cold." Glory said.

I eyed her earmuffs. I didn't know if I could find earmuffs, but I needed a knit hat to keep my ears warm.

Glory zipped her jacket and handed Isabella a small silver counter. "Isabella," Glory said. "Why don't you keep track of the people you two talk to?" Glory turned to me, "We use it for the program's data collecting."

My stomach burned. Did Glory think I couldn't be trusted to keep track of the people? Isabella wasn't even talking to guests!

Isabella smiled and took the small metal object. She clicked it twice for the two people I had already talked to. As soon as Glory moved away, Isabella pulled her phone back out and kept texting. Occasionally, she glanced up and clicked on the clicker a few times. The insides of my stomach burned stronger. This wasn't the way you collected data!

I spent the next hour talking to people about the tide pools. Isabella alternated between clicking and scrolling on her cell phone. The crowds continued to gather around Martina and Angelina, and Glory manned the truck, so no one was really watching Isabella. I didn't want to get everyone upset on my first day as a junior SEALS by tattling on Isabella, but I knew that what she was doing wasn't helping the SEALS program, and she wasn't following the rules. Isabella's random clicks weren't collecting the right numbers of visitors we were talking to, and the SEALS program probably needed those numbers to give to important people—like people who gave them money for the truck and supplies.

When I looked over at her, she smiled at me and clicked. I gritted my teeth.

As the tide turned and lapped at the rocks, filling up the tide pools, Glory waded into the tide pools and grabbed the sandwich board. Angelina and Martina picked up the signs stuck in the sand as the water pooled around them. Isabella stood beside me and I lifted the painted signs from the trailer and stored them inside. She clicked the clicker at me as if she was telling me to hurry up.

When I was done, I slipped off my jacket and dropped it into the bin in the truck. I dropped my nametag into the black basket. SEALS junior volunteer wasn't exactly what I thought.

"Thanks for your help." Glory dropped her arm around my shoulder. "See you next Saturday, okay?"

"Sure." I exhaled loudly.

"I'll be here too!" Isabella said. "We can volunteer at the tide pools again! It was so much fun!"

I clenched my fists. I did not want to volunteer with Isabella next Saturday.

"Do you want a ride?" Glory asked me as Isabella, Martina and Angelina piled into the cab of the truck.

"I'll walk." I didn't want to spend a minute more with Isabella.

Glory turned the truck toward the ramp on the south end of the beach. Isabella sat in the front beside Glory. Angelina and Martina sat together in the back seat of the cab.

Glory stuck her hand out the window and waved in a three-finger wave.

I gave her a three-finger wave. I hoped she didn't notice my wave was a little clumsy. I'd have to practice to get it to look like hers.

Isabella gave me a big wave like we were the best of friends. "See you next week!" She hollered out the truck window.

The velella velella slipped under my feet and I stomped on them with a satisfying squash.

7
STEAM CLUB

*O*n Monday at school, Mr. Carson instructed us to get our Chromebooks from the classroom cart. He pointed to a small chart attached to the white board and reminded everyone that we were two points away from earning a free period. Mr. Carson liked to encourage what he called collaborative learning, which meant we had to do a lot of assignments in partners or with our table groups. After the visit to Sea Rock, each table group had to create a visual which represented what we had seen and learned. My table group was working on a poster-size drawing. I thought it would have been fun to do a slide show on the computer, but both Martina and Sofia voted no and since there were just three of us, I was outvoted.

"Why don't we include the scientific names too?" I asked as Martina colored Sea Rock with a brown watercolor pencil. The pencil set doubled as both colored pencils and watercolor paints. I had never seen colored pencils that were also watercolors. But so far, Martina hadn't let me try it.

Martina set down the pencil and picked up a watercolor

brush. She squeezed water from a plastic tube onto the poster. It spread onto the brown pencil shading, making it look like she'd used watercolors instead of colored pencils. "The drawing will be too cluttered if we use all those long names."

"I could type the names and we could paste them on."

"We don't want the names typed." Sofia turned to Martina. "Right?" The two had obviously picked out matching outfits. Both of them wore red Pelican Elementary School hooded sweatshirts and dark denim jeans with a rip across the knee, so when they sat, their knees stuck out from their jeans. Sofia had a soft pink lip gloss on her lips and a red headband kept her hair out of her face. During lunch, Sofia braided Martina's hair into a long braid and swept it up across the back of her head. Martina wore the same pink lip gloss as Sofia.

"Right," Martina said, in the exact same tone as Sofia. "This is an art project. We want everything to be drawn like the panels on the SEALS trailer."

I had to admit the panels on the SEALS trailer were fabulous, and we would get a good grade on our project.

A burst of laughter erupted across the room. Mr. Carson stood over a table of boys who jostled each other and one landed on the floor in a thump. As much as I didn't like Martina and Sofia, I really didn't want to be partnered with boys. Most of the boys just wanted to play games on their computer tablets. At least Martina and Sofia cared about their grades.

"We really don't need all of us working on this project." Sofia sketched a green anemone in what I guessed was supposed to be the tide pools. She didn't look up at me. "You could work on homework or something. We don't mind."

I grabbed my backpack and yanked out my free reading book for language arts and pretended to read. It was a book by Rachel Carson about the sea that I'd found at the library. Mr.

Carson said the language was very poetic and I should keep a journal of phrases and words I liked. But I couldn't see the blurry words as I blinked hard to keep away the tears.

I looked up and stared at the daily schedule posted in colorful strips of paper on the whiteboard. In the morning class meeting, Mr. Carson always went over the daily schedule and moved the little strips around. Sometimes we had library. Sometimes PE. And sometimes music. We always had free choice at the end of the day. Free choice was the worst part of the day. Mr. Carson said it was a good time to get caught up, and we could work in the centers, wrapping up morning work, practicing vocabulary games on the Chromebooks or reading in the reading corner. But most people just played games on the Chromebooks or talked, usually loudly, in small groups. Mr. Carson didn't seem to mind and sometimes played internet games too.

During free choice, I tried to research on the internet. I was keeping notes on all the oceanology websites I used in my research of sea stars. So far, I had discovered there were ten different kinds of sea stars on the Oregon Coast. I had tried to ask a couple people walking around town about the sea stars but no one really knew much about them.

But, instead of free choice, Mr. Carson told us today was Club Day and he wanted to surprise us. Everyone cheered as he changed the daily schedule on the whiteboard and there was a quick scramble as kids packed up bags and headed to clubs. I wasn't sure what to do. A group of kids were streaming into the room, mobbing Mr. Carson with questions about games and grabbing our class set of Chromebooks. I guessed he must be the online games club advisor.

"Lucy!" Mr. Carson peered over the group of kids clustered around him at his document-camera cart. "Sorry about that—I forgot you haven't done Club Day with us! We do it a couple times a month. How does STEAM Club sound to you? It's a club where you study science, technology, engineering, art and math."

STEAM was perfect! Maybe someone would want to talk about the sea stars. I crossed my fingers that Sofia and Martina did not go to STEAM club.

Mr. Carson consulted a clipboard attached to a small peg behind his desk. "Portable one. Out the main doors of the school and take a right. First portable on your left."

I grabbed my bag and headed down the hall, following Martina and Sofie. Their matching brown sandals with silver and gold beads clip-clopped on the linoleum floor. When we reached the cafeteria, both turned to go inside. At least ten other kids, who looked to be mostly fourth and fifth graders, clustered around one of the circular tables. A tall woman, who I was pretty sure was one of the fourth grade teachers, wore a long white apron with her hair tied up in a cluster on top of her head, stood at the table with small bread pans spread in front of her.

I headed out the school's double doors and turned to the portables. Portable one had a ramp leading up to the door. I pulled open the heavy door and when I stepped inside, I could tell it was one of the special education rooms. A rocking chair sat in the corner beside a small bookcase of picture books. Baskets of very easy reading books about skills like brushing your teeth and washing your hands sat on the top. Rubber bouncy balls, an assortment of walkers, and a wheelchair sat in the far left corner of the portable, and one entire corner had been dedicated as a nap safe zone with thick pillows, yoga mats, and a couple of blue blankets. A teacher's desk sat by the window and above the window was a banner: "Everyone is special."

Suddenly, the door opened again and Kyra from the

SEALS program stepped inside, pushing a boy in a wheel-chair. He had short blonde hair in a bowl cut and wore jeans, work boots and a flannel shirt. A camera hung around his neck and he held a notebook on his lap.

"Lucy!" Kyra said. "Sorry we're late. This is Devon." Kyra leaned down to eye-level with Devon. She increased the volume of her voice and spoke slowly. "I will pick you up after clubs, okay?"

Devon rolled his eyes. "I'm in a wheelchair, Kyra. I didn't lose my hearing."

"Brothers." Kyra rolled her eyes, knelt and gave him a kiss on his forehead which he shrugged off and in one quick turn of his chair, he faced me. "Who are you?'

"Lucy Lavender. I'm new."

"Mmmm …" Devon eyed me.

I wasn't sure what the "mmmm …" meant. Was it a good sound or bad? "Why aren't you in school?" I asked.

"Because," he said, pronouncing every syllable as if I was slow, "I am in this wheelchair."

I shrugged and motioned toward the ramp he had just come up and the wheelchair in the room. "Wheelchairs don't stop you from going to school." I placed my hands on my hips. "How come you don't go to school?"

"I go to school online," Devon said. He shook his head like I should have known, and a small tsk came out of his mouth. "I come to school for enrichment opportunities."

I raised my right eyebrow. Who said "enrichment opportunities" unless you were a teacher? Was this the way he talked or was he doing it on purpose because he thought he was smarter than me.

The sound of wheels rolling on the ramp broke my thoughts, and then Autumn opened the door, pulling a black suitcase that looked like she was going away on a two-month trip somewhere. I bet it would never pass the weight restrictions at the airport.

"Hey, everyone." Autumn wore heavy hiking boots, a long patchwork skirt, a blue sweater with red and yellow hearts stitched along the cuffs and a red lace scarf tied at her neck. Her hair hung in long curly waves around her face and she wore bright red lipstick. She wore a school badge that said Volunteer, and she didn't have any of her SEALS badges or coats with her.

"Is this STEAM Club?" I asked.

"I thought this was photography club," Devon said. "That's what I signed up for."

"You're in luck!" Autumn dropped the suitcase so it lay face up on the ground. "It's STEAM club, with the "A" for art! Photography is art."

"But where is everyone else?" I fiddled with a strap on my backpack. I had never been in a club with just one other person. It seemed like if the whole school was doing clubs, then there should be more people here.

"Sports club, mostly." Autumn shook her head and pointed to the grassy field filled with kids just beyond the portables. "I have no idea why everyone would choose to go to sports club. It's going to pour rain any minute." As if on cue, small sprinkles of water splashed against the portable window.

"What are we going to do today?" Devon asked. "Lucy doesn't have a camera." He peered out the window. "And if it's raining, I don't want to get wet."

"What ideas do you have for us, Genius?" Autumn hoisted herself on top of the teacher's desk and swung her legs back and forth. She smiled at Devon. "I am all ears."

I didn't think it was fair Devon should direct what we did in STEAM club. I was the scientist. "We could make a study of the sea stars," I said before Devon could answer. I pulled out my notebook. I hoped to steer us back to the science part of the club.

"Go on." Autumn twirled a thread on her scarf.

"The first thing to do when trying to study a species is to count how many there are, so you know what has changed over time. We could go to Sea Rock and count the sea stars."

Autumn eyed me and stopped twirling her scarf thread. "I like your idea. But I have to get permission to take you two in the car to Sea Rock. Let me work on that and we'll do something else today."

"What's in your suitcase?" Devon wheeled over to the suitcase.

"I'm glad you asked." Autumn hopped off the desk and unzipped her canvas suitcase. Plastic molds filled the suitcase. There were molds in shapes of seahorses, seashells, sea stars, and even octopuses. Tucked around the plastic molds were various sized see-through bags filled with microplastics, small bits of rope and plastic bottle caps. Autumn pulled out a bottle of what looked like glue and placed it on the desk. She pushed back her sleeve and revealed a colorful blue and green plastic bracelet encircling her wrist.

"What's on your wrist?" I peered closer.

"Beach trash treasures." Autumn moved her hair away from her ears, and green and yellow sea urchins appeared, dangling from thin wires.

"You made that with the molds?" I picked up one of the molds which had the same design as the earrings.

"Yep," Autumn said.

Beach trash treasures wasn't what I thought of as fancy art, but it was interesting.

"I'm not really into making jewelry," Devon said. "How about I take pictures? We can document the process and I'll post the pictures to a website I make for our club?'

"Good idea!" I snapped my fingers. "We can make people aware of the beach trash and how it harms the environment when animals eat it!"

Devon reached into a tan pouch attached to the back of his wheelchair. He hoisted out a laptop computer and booted it up. "I've got a ton of pictures and ideas," he said. "I've already made two websites about octopuses."

"You like octopuses?" I asked.

Devon shrugged. "I think they're kinda fun, how they can slip in and out of places and get out of their water crates at the aquarium." He waved his arms around in the air. "I'd like to do that too. I'd slip right out of this chair and go wherever I wanted."

I giggled. I'd like to be an octopus too.

"Good," Autumn said, and smiled at us. "So both of you are on board."

I was more than on board. For the first time since I had started Pelican Elementary something like hope bubbled inside me. Devon liked science. He liked marine science just like me.

"The first thing we need to do is sort the beach trash by colors." Autumn held up three trays with dividers. "We'll sort everything into here."

"Some of it is really big," I waved a piece of turquoise rope in the air.

"When we fill the molds," Autumn said. "we will cut the pieces to fit into the molds." Autumn reached in and grabbed the rope. She dropped it into the trash can beside her. "Or throw it away."

We both pulled on gloves and for the next thirty minutes, Autumn and I sorted while Devon took pictures, mostly just of our hands and of the small pieces of trash. Sometimes he would stop and fiddle with some buttons on his computer.

When everything was sorted, Autumn plunked the molds in front of us. "Next, we fill the molds with the pieces of trash. We'll use the resin to fill around each item in the mold. It'll take a couple days to dry. Next club meeting, in another week or so, we can drill some holes for the necklace wires and earrings."

I picked up a mold of sea stars. "I'm going to make a lot of these. Scientists always need money for their research. Maybe we can sell the jewelry to make money for sea star research and bring awareness to the sea star's wasting syndrome."

"I can build us a website for that!" Devon said, and clicked furiously on his computer. "This will be really fun!"

The hour passed quickly and by four o'clock we had a row of filled molds sitting on the ledge by the windowsill. Autumn said we'd have to carry them to Mr. Carson's classroom so they could dry.

I took two and carried them like a waitress balancing meals. Devon placed one on his lap and Autumn took three. We walked down the ramp and toward the school. Devon used the small ramp leading up to the school and Autumn and I walked up the stairs. The smell of spiced bread drifted from the cafeteria. Sofia and Martina walked out of the doors of the cafeteria. Each carried a small wrapped bread loaf.

My stomach rumbled. Lunch seemed like a long time ago, and whatever Mom and I were having for dinner tonight wasn't going to taste as good as homemade bread. Today was food closet day, so we'd at least have a choice of things for dinner, unlike the end of the month when all we usually had left was boxes of ramen and a few odd cans of vegetables and fruits. Even though Mom had a job now, we hadn't been at the cottages long enough for Mom to get a check and Mom said we'd use the food pantry for a few more weeks, until she got paid.

Sofia stopped in front of Devon. "Hi, Devon." She smiled at him in what could only be called a flirting smile. "Would you like a piece of bread?"

Devon shook his head and his ears reddened. "No, thank you."

"Okay," Sofia said in a soft voice. "Maybe next time."

She and Martina slipped into the office where they offered Sofia's mom and two teachers bread. All three of them nodded their heads and Ms. Gabriella opened a cabinet and brought out a stack of napkins.

A group of boys entered from the back doors of the school, tossing a football between them. The football sailed up and over Devon's head and bounced on the hall floor.

"Hey, Devon," one of the boys muttered while the others hurried around Devon as if he wasn't there, chasing the ball.

Devon pressed the button on his wheelchair and spun ahead of me. "Wait!" I hurried to catch up to him.

"I thought you just came to clubs," I said. "But you know Sofia and those boys."

"I used to go to school here before the accident." Devon stared straight ahead of him.

"What happened?" I asked.

"I was playing soccer," Devon said. "My spine got injured. Those were my friends." He nodded to the group of boys rounding the corner and heading into Mr. Carson's classroom. "Here." He shoved the molds toward me. "I'm not going into the classroom."

"I can't carry all these!" The molds I held threatened to spill out of my hands and land in a gooey mess in the hallway.

Autumn stepped up behind me and grabbed mine from me. She placed my filled molds on the floor and took Devon's. "I'll take yours and come back for the others." Autumn strode forward in that step that said she didn't mess around and was all business. I had a feeling she was going to have a few words with Mr. Carson about the boys in the hallway.

Devon whirled his wheelchair around in the direction of the door.

I ran after him.

He stopped at the door and hit the button on the left. The doors didn't open.

Sofia dashed out of the office and held open one of the double doors for Devon. She tossed her hair as he wheeled past her and it was easy to see she had applied new lip gloss. But unlike all the adults who loved Sofia and thanked her for everything, Devon didn't thank her as he wheeled down the small ramp and toward a set of bushes alongside the building. A few seconds later his sister, Kyra, pulled up into the circular area for waiting cars and loaded Devon and his wheelchair into the car.

I waved as they drove past me. "Bye Devon!" I wanted him to know that I wasn't like the hallway boys. I wasn't like Sofia who had a crush on him. I liked Devon because he liked science, just like me, and I wanted to be his friend.

8

THE BOOK SHOP

When I got home from school, Mom had left a note saying she was at City Hall getting some paperwork straightened out and she'd be back soon to go to the food closet together. Everywhere we lived, we always went to the food closets. Sometimes they were big rooms with helpful women wearing colorful aprons, with lots of fresh fruits and vegetables. Other times they were small rooms with canned food on shelves, the spaces between them so small we could barely squeeze by.

A half-eaten bag of dog food sat on our kitchen counter. Cottage guests left all kinds of things; Mom had a whole collection of jackets and sweatshirts in a big laundry basket by the door. Most of the items had been in the basket from guests before we arrived. She said we could sort through the basket at the end of each month if no one claimed the items. I had my eye on a heavy hooded rain jacket that would be perfect for SEALS.

I folded the dog food bag and placed a piece of tape across the top. I packed the bag into my backpack and hopped on my bike and headed toward the restaurant where I'd seen Thomas playing his guitar last Saturday. Small droplets of rain fell on my arms and head. It wasn't one of the rain gushers yet, so I kept going.

When I pedaled past the crooked art gallery building, Aunt Charlotte stood in the doorway. Her back was to me, but her voice carried outside and sounded upset. It looked like she was having an argument with the man inside. Did she order art and it wasn't ready? Or had she bought something that she didn't like and wanted to return it? I couldn't really imagine people getting upset with artists. Artists created things which made people happy. The Lab lay on the porch and stared at the doorway.

I pressed hard on my pedals and zipped past. Aunt Charlotte had tried to call Mom a couple of times in the last week, but Mom usually let it go to voice mail. So far, she hadn't stopped by to visit with us. I didn't want her to see me and remind her that a visit would be a good idea.

When I reached the dog shop, I leaned my bike against the building and walked inside. Samantha, the owner, was hanging canvas bags on a small hook. Her dark hair was gathered into a ponytail under a cap with the name of the fancy restaurant across the street stitched in yellow across the front.

"Have you seen Thomas and Luna?"

Samantha shook her head. "I haven't seen him for a few days. He missed a big crowd for brunch on Sunday."

"Do you know where he might be? I have something for Luna." I patted my backpack.

Samantha smiled at me and said, "Check the bookstore at the end of the street. He likes to hang out there when it's raining." Samantha reached under the counter. She pulled out a bone. "I've been saving this for Luna if you want to take it to her."

"Thanks." I slipped the bone in my backpack and scurried out the door. It was Luna's lucky day. I rode my bike down to the end of the street. The rain had picked up and slanted sideways across my cheeks, and I shivered. I hoped the bookshop was warm.

When I reached the bookshop, I parked my bike in an empty bike rack and ducked inside. A heavyset man with a dark beard sat on a tall stool by the counter. He wore a flannel shirt, jeans and sandals, and flipped through a small paperback book. His glasses perched at the end of his nose, and dark curly hair swirled across his forehead. A fat black and white tuxedo cat lay across the counter. Her tail swished but her eyes remained closed.

"Welcome," the man said. "I'm Judson, the owner. Can I help you find something?"

"I found him," I nodded toward Thomas who sat in a plush denim armchair with a hole ripped in the left side. The armchair sat beside one of those fake gas fireplaces that blew warm air into the room. Luna lay by his side, her eyes closed. The cat didn't seem fazed by Luna lying on the floor and Luna didn't seem bothered by the cat.

"Thomas!" I said. "I was looking for you!"

Luna raised her head and wagged her tail. The cat opened her eyes and studied me. I knelt on the thin-carpeted floor and pet Luna. Her tail wagged even more.

"You were looking for me?" Thomas raised an eyebrow. He placed his paperback book upside down on the arm of his chair.

"Yes." I grabbed my bag from my shoulders. "I have something for Luna." I pulled out the bag of dog food. "A guest left it in the cottages."

Thomas's eyes lit up. "That's a really good brand. Grain

free. Luna doesn't usually get food like that." He took the bag from me. "Thank you."

I gave him the bone Samantha had given me at the dog shop. "This is for Luna, too. From Samantha."

Thomas tucked the bone into his shirt pocket. "I'll give this to her a little later." He reached into a black bag at his side. "And I have something for you." Thomas pulled out a worn paperback book and handed it to me.

I turned it over. *The Sea Around Us* by Rachel Carson.

"I know this book." I ran my fingers over the blue and white cover with a picture of a sea wave and white foam.

Thomas's face fell. "You do? I thought it might be one you hadn't read yet."

"I mean I'm reading the first book in this series." I didn't want Thomas to think I didn't appreciate his gift. It was very thoughtful.

"So, you haven't read this one?" Thomas said, his voice bright.

"No." I clutched the book to my chest. "Thank you."

"Come on." Thomas stood and guided me to a collection of marine books. He pulled down a copy of another book by Rachel Carson, *The Edge of the Sea.* "That's the third book in the series."

I sat cross-legged on the floor in the marine science book section. I flipped through marine coloring books, resource guides that looked like college texts and thick books about working on the sea. I'd never seen such a collection of sea and marine books, not even at the library.

"Where did all these come from?" I looked up.

Thomas had disappeared, but Judson heard me from his perch on the stool. "People give them to me in trade for other books," he said. "Everyone reads around here and ends up with quite a collection of books. "He chuckled. "Rain will do that for you—make you a reader."

"My Dad grew up in Sea Rock Cove," I said and fingered the sea star necklace. "His name was Rick Lavender. He wasn't really a reader." Dad liked to watch movies. He watched all kinds of movies. Documentaries. Award winners. Movies with car chases and movies with love scenes. Dad liked them all.

Judson nodded. "Not everyone likes to read. But stories are stories no matter how they are told."

"Did you know my Dad?"

Judson shook his head. "I took over this bookstore from my grandma. I grew up north of Seattle, but when I was a child, we visited Sea Rock Cove every summer for at least a month. When she passed away, I inherited the shop." He shrugged. "No one in the family really wanted to take on a used bookstore."

When Dad died, I hadn't inherited anything. But living in Sea Rock Cove felt like I was closer to Dad. A lot closer, almost like I had inherited his town.

A collection of children's books filled four bookshelves by the back window. Mom loved children's books. She lost her collection in a house fire when she was seventeen and she was always dragging me into bookstores to show me which books she'd once owned. I made my way over to the children's section and thumbed through *Heidi, A Little Princess,* and fairy tales by Hans Christian Andersen. The books all looked to be about thirty years old or more. There was an entire collection of Little Golden Books. I knew exactly where to go for Mom's gifts.

"I've got picture books the library hasn't had for years," Judson said. "Do you want me to get some out of the back?"

"Maybe later." I didn't have any money to get Mom a present right now. "Do you know where Thomas is?" Luna still lay in her spot by the chair. She had rolled over and a light snore drifted over from her.

Judson nodded toward a section of books labeled fantasy.

I stepped around a corner of tall shelves. Thomas was sprawled on a thick carpet. A stack of books by a man named Terry Brooks was at his feet.

"Have you read all those?" I asked.

"Yes. I'm looking for the next one in the Magic Kingdom of Landover series. It's not as popular as his Shannara series and I have a hard time finding them. But Judson gets them in sometimes." Thomas suddenly cried out and held up a dusty copy of a thick book with a black and gold cover. "Here it is!

Thomas rose to his feet with his book in hand. He scooped the other books on the floor up and carefully put them into the right alphabetical order in the bookshelf. He walked to the counter, limping a bit on his left side.

Judson waved his hand. "Keep it. This one is on me."

"Nah," Thomas dug out change from his pocket and a couple of dollar bills. "Here you go."

I knew exactly how Thomas felt. Mom and I always made sure to pay for things. We didn't like people giving us charity and feeling sorry for us.

Thomas clipped Luna to her leash. "Time to go, Luna."

"I better go, too," I said to Judson. I didn't know what time it was but it felt like I'd been in the bookstore for a long time.

"Come back anytime." Judson dunked a tea bag into a bright blue mug that said, *Sea Rock Cove Sandcastle Contest.* A picture of Sea Rock was printed on the front and tufted puffins sat on the top of Sea Rock. The picture looked a lot like the art panels I hung on the SEALS trailer, with the same style and design.

"Did the man in the art gallery make that?" I pointed to the picture.

"Sure thing." Judson dropped his tea bag onto a small plate. "Max always makes the art for all our festivals."

Max. The man in the art gallery's name was Max, the same name as on the panels on the SEALS trailers.

I followed Thomas out the door and grabbed my bike.

"Thomas," I said. "Who is Max?"

Thomas stopped as Luna sniffed a bush. "Max? Long-time resident of Sea Rock Cove. Owned the town's biggest hotel at one point. Owned three hotels up and down the Oregon Coast. Sold everything about twelve years ago and bought that building so he could have a place to sell his art."

"Sofia and Martina said something happened to him. They were afraid of him and said no one in the town talks to him. But I saw Aunt Charlotte inside his art gallery talking to him." I didn't tell Thomas that Aunt Charlotte looked like she was yelling at him.

"Well," Thomas said as he tugged on Luna's leash and guided her away from sniffing at a small bunny nestled among the rhododendrons. "I guess your aunt isn't everyone, is she?"

"But what happened to him?" I pressed Thomas. "Sofia said something happened to him."

"Some stories are not mine to tell, Lucy Lavender," Thomas said as a police car slowed and stopped beside us.

I swallowed. The police could be friendly at school when they gave talks about not talking to strangers and telling someone if you were getting hurt at home or at school. But sometimes they were scary. The police cleaned up the house-less camps in Portland that Mom and I sometimes parked near for a few nights. Mom always started the car right away and drove to the nearest Burger Town. We pretended to go inside to get dinner, but instead headed for the restroom and waited until the police left the camps. Was Thomas in trouble? Had Mom gotten worried because I didn't leave a note and it was getting late? Did she call the police to look for me?

The officer opened his door and got out. A German shepherd sitting in the back seat. The car said K-9.

Luna lurched at the car and snarled at the German shepherd.

Thomas pulled hard on her leash and away from the police car. "Afternoon, Officer Fredricks," he said.

"Afternoon." Officer Fredricks walked over to us. He had blonde hair and bright blue eyes and was about medium build. A gold wedding ring was on his ring finger and he looked to be somewhere in his forties. He nodded to me. "You're Lucy Lavender." his voice was deep and strong.

I fiddled with the handlebars on my bike. Mom must have called him. I was in trouble. "I'm sorry," I said. "I'm going right home. I should have left a note for Mom but I just wanted to see Thomas and Luna and give them the bag of dog food."

Office Fredricks chuckled. "It's okay," he said. "Your mom didn't call me. I know who you are because it's my job to know when someone new moves into town. I want to keep everyone safe."

"Oh," I exhaled. Office Fredricks must be a good policeman.

"But," he winked at me, "maybe you should start heading for home just in case your mom starts worrying."

"I'm on my way," I said. "I was just waiting for it to stop raining." I raised my hand to the sky. "It looks like it's stopped!"

Officer Fredricks turned to Thomas. "Thomas, I haven't seen you around for a few days."

"Had some business in Seaman Point," Thomas said and shook his head. "It took me a while to get back."

Seaman Point was about forty minutes north of Sea Rock

Cove. There was a bus that stopped three times a day at the station two blocks from the cottages. I wasn't sure why it would take Thomas a couple days to get back.

"Everything okay?" Officer Fredricks leaned back against the car. He tapped his fingers on the door.

Thomas shifted back and forth on his feet. "Could have been better."

Officer Fredricks looked like he wanted to say something, but the computer perched on his passenger seat beeped. He eyed the screen. "I need to go. I'll find you later, okay?"

Officer Fredricks got back in the car and pulled away. He turned on his lights without the siren.

"You better get going, Lucy Lavender," Thomas said.

I nodded and hopped on my bike. "Thanks for the book!" I patted my backpack and waved to Thomas. I pedaled toward home as the questions crashed in my head. What was Thomas doing in Seaman Point? And why wouldn't he tell me anything more about Max? I vowed to find out.

9

BLACK OYSTERCATCHERS

*O*n Saturday morning, I walked by the hotel with the puffin statue on my way to Junior SEALS. Someone needed to paint black over the white chest. Maybe that could be an "A" for art project for STEAM Club. I climbed up and over the built-up sand dune and slid down like I was coming down a big mountain on a sled. There was a lot of discussion about the sand dunes in Sea Rock Cove. Some people liked them and said they protected people from king tides and the possibility of a tsunami. They called the dunes the first line of defense if the unthinkable big wave were to happen. But other people wanted the dunes to be graded so they could see the ocean better, which meant huge trucks would come and cart the sand to other places along the shoreline. I thought the dunes were fun.

The SEALS truck was parked in front of Sea Rock. A crowd of people milled among the tide pools. I was late and hoped I wouldn't get in trouble. Mom had needed me to watch things while she ran up to the bakery to get some pastries. Mom liked to offer pastries to the guests. Most didn't take them and preferred to go to the local coffee shop, which was known for its special brewed coffee and berry scones. But a few guests were grateful they could have a pastry while they packed up and headed out. Mom said that's what it was all about when you ran a lodging place—you had to think of all the guests' needs, and they never needed the same thing.

When I reached the tide pools, the tide was pretty far out. I checked the board in the back of the SEALS truck and it said today was a minus 1.5 tide at 10:00 a.m. The summer had the lowest tides of the year in what were called minus tides. It was when the tide went out further than usual. A lot of things got exposed, and people could walk right up to the edges of Sea Rock. I'd heard that sometimes the tide was so low you could walk all the way around Sea Rock. Clusters of people gathered around the right side where a handful of sea stars had been exposed. Not like the amount of sea stars Dad used to see, and I'd seen in photos, but enough that I could tell there were still some sea stars at Sea Rock, which was a good thing.

At the base of Sea Rock, Glory held a thick rope in her hands and there was another one stretched across the lower base. I walked around the tide pools and toward her as a black bird with an orange bill cried in short piercing sounds. A black oystercatcher. It was hard to miss them, with the bright ring of orange surrounding their eyes and their piercing cries. Black oystercatchers were considered a species of concern because of their small population and low nesting success rate on the Oregon Coast. The birds had long orange beaks that they used to prod among the rocks in the intertidal zone, looking for food such as mussels and limpets. A second black oystercatcher perched on a small rock shelf above the lower edges of the exposed intertidal area and chirped even louder.

"What's going on?" I asked Glory, above the short, sharp calls.

"Grab the rope," Glory said. "We've got to get this area marked off."

The birds continued to chirp loudly as we worked. A crowd gathered behind us. Glory yelled, "Stay back! The black oystercatchers have a nest."

I peered closer. I knew it was important to keep people away from the black oystercatchers' nest. Unlike the other nesting birds of Sea Rock, they built their nests low where it was easy to be disturbed by humans. If people scared the birds off the nest area, then predators like the gulls would get the young chicks. This was part of the reason why their nesting success rate—the number of nests that managed to hatch at least one egg—was so low.

"I don't see anything," I said.

"Look to the left side. One chick is already gone. People scared the adult oystercatchers off last night when we weren't here."

The SEALS were only on the beach during daylight hours, at low tide. Sometimes that was two times a day and sometimes it was only once, but they weren't ever on the beach at night. If the low tide happened at night, no one was there to protect the black oystercatchers' nest.

Glory's face darkened. "This is the third year this has happened. People get close and the birds fly off, and then their nests are vulnerable to predators like the gulls and eagle. Sometimes I feel like we should camp out here all night."

I pictured Thomas and Luna lying on the sand beside Sea Rock. He said he liked to spend the night on the beach sometimes, even if camping wasn't allowed on the beach. No one would bother the black oystercatchers. "I know someone who might be up for the job."

Glory finished roping off the area. "You do?"

"Yeah," I said. "I'll ask him." I didn't tell Glory who I was going to ask because I wasn't sure how she felt about Thomas. But the important thing was protecting the black oyster-catchers.

"Where do you want me to go today?" I asked Glory. I hadn't seen any sign of Isabella, but she said she'd be here, and I wanted to be far away from her. At the tide pools, Angelina talked to a group of women and Martina stood next to her. Both peered into the tide pools, showing the women the giant green anemones.

"Stand on the side with the black oystercatcher nest," Glory said. "Stay far enough away that the birds aren't chirping at you, but close enough to warn the people who want to get too close."

Glory finished giving instructions and strode toward the other side of Sea Rock. A group of people gathered and tried to remove the rope line. The black oystercatchers' cries filled the air. Martina and Angelina looked up, excused themselves from the tide pools and made their way toward the black oystercatchers and where I was standing.

"Excuse me," I said to the group near the rope. "You're too close to the birds!"

The family of what looked like grandparents, children, parents and siblings stepped closer instead of away. One of the children ducked under the rope. Frustrated, I yelled louder. "You're too close to the birds!"

Martina quickly stepped toward them and said,

"*Disculpe, les pido por favor que se alejen del nido de las aves.*"

"*No nos dimos cuenta, perdón.*" The family apologized, pulled the child back from under the rope and moved away.

"They don't speak English," I said, understanding dawning. The family hadn't been ignoring me. They couldn't under-stand me.

"People speak lots of different languages," Martina said in

her soft, quiet voice. "That's why my cousin helps out. She can interpret a lot of languages, not only Spanish but also some Russian and French."

Glory strode back to us. "What was that about?"

Angelina quickly explained what had happened.

After Angelina explained, Glory nodded to Martina. "Good job. Can you and Angelina go back to the tide pools? I'll stay here with Lucy."

I waited for Glory to tell me good job too, but instead she only said, "You forgot your name tag," and pointed to the truck. "They're in the bin on the left side of the trailer."

I scurried across the sand and to the truck. I really wanted Glory to like me and forgetting my name tag wasn't winning points. I opened up the right door of the truck and scrounged through the bin on the back seat to find my name tag. I found it and slipped the bin back inside and shut the door.

As I turned to head back to Glory, Max and his dog walked toward the truck. He carried a white trash bag and every once in a while, leaned over and picked up another plastic bottle or dog poop bag someone had left by the driftwood fire logs scattered along the beach.

He nodded at me. "Morning," he said, his voice gruff. His dog sniffed at the wheel of the truck. He placed the full bag of trash inside the truck bed.

Did Autumn sift through the trash Max brought in for the beach trash jewelry? His bag looked like it had a lot more in it than the small microplastics. But maybe she made other things out of beach trash besides jewelry.

"Good morning," I said in my polite voice. "What's your dog's name?"

"Honeybear," Max said. "Honeybear helps me on my morning walk picking up trash."

The dog sniffed the side of the truck. Honeybear seemed

like such a funny name for Max's dog when Max himself was so reclusive and sometimes a little scary. I had expected his dog to have a name like Charger or Fang. But I had to admit, now that I knew the dog's name and Max was talking to me, he didn't seem as threatening as he had last Saturday when I'd seen him on the beach. Sometimes just knowing names helped make everything seem a little less intimidating.

I wanted to pet Honeybear, but before I could ask Max if I could pet his dog, she moved away from me and sniffed at the back tire of the truck. Max moved with her, so they were standing further away from me. He had been polite, but he still didn't have that welcoming attitude that made it seem like he wanted a twelve-year-old following him and his dog around the truck.

I told myself to observe Max like I would a science experiment. I studied his height and noted he must be almost five eleven or so. Dad had been tall like that too. Max had a thin build and a narrow face. He wore a knit cap and a deep green heavy jacket over dark blue denim jeans, not any different than most of the locals who I saw walking their dogs on the beach, dressed for the cold spring weather.

"Do I pass the test?" he asked me, and a small smile darted across his face.

I flushed, embarrassed to be caught studying him so closely.

Max turned and stared at Sea Rock. "I like to observe too. I come out here and study the same section of Sea Rock for hours, trying to note all the colors and the way the light moves across it." He turned and pointed to the hillside behind us. "When the sun comes up in the morning and the birds all fly off Sea Rock, it's one of the best times to be here."

"Do you ever see the bunnies on the beach?" I had seen them on the pathways leading to the beach and in the dunes, but I hadn't seen them on the beach itself. Maybe bunnies didn't like the ocean and were afraid to get too close to the water.

"Nope," Max shook his head. "Never seen them out here on the beach.

"They are all over the yards at the cottages that my mom manages," I said. "They're kinda a problem for the guests with dogs. Are they a problem for Honeybear?"

Max shrugged. "She doesn't mind them. I just give her a good tug on the leash and keep her close to me when we walk by them. Whatever you do, don't poison them."

"Poison them?" Who would poison the bunnies? We didn't like them but we would never poison them.

"Some people really don't want them around. They can get into the yard beds and really play havoc with things. A while back, it was rumored that a few folks tried to poison them. That didn't go over too well."

"No." I shuddered, not even wanting to think about how the bunnies could be poisoned. They were nuisances, but surely there were other ways to lower their population.

"What brings you out to Sea Rock?" Max asked. His eyes searched my face. "Not everyone wants to volunteer out here in the cold and rain. Takes a special kind of person."

"I am studying the sea stars." I yanked the necklace out of the inside of my shirt. "My dad gave this to me. He loved the sea stars and had a tattoo of a sea star. I want to be a marine biologist."

Max's face darkened as if a storm had taken over it. He stiffened and looked away from me. I stepped back as an intensity radiated off him. Had I said something wrong? I heard the words of Sofia and Martina ringing in my ears: "Something happened to him." I knew about something happening to people. Sometimes Mom and I ran into people who had something happen to them and they seemed a little scary. At those times, Mom said it was best if we just kept on moving in the opposite direction.

I thought it might be best now if I just kept moving in the opposite direction. The only problem was that Max and Honeybear had moved, so in order for me to get to the black oystercatchers, I would have to move closer to them.

"Lucy!" Isabella tapped my shoulder. "I'm here!" She said it as though we were best friends and I had been waiting for her, which of course I hadn't, but right at that moment, I was really glad to see her.

Isabella held up a bulging patchwork bag. "I brought lunch to share with you!" Isabella wore a different cap today, but her hair was still in a ponytail sticking out the back. She had on similar jeans to Sofia and Martina, with the rip across the knee, and a blue hooded sweatshirt.

I gritted my teeth. Even if I was glad to see Isabella right now, the last thing I wanted to do was eat lunch with her. "Martina is here." I pointed toward the tide pools. "She might like to eat with you."

"Oh no." Isabella shook her head. "Martina and Angelina always eat together. Angelina brings food from the restaurant where she works. She just brings enough for the two of them and they have private talks." She raised her right eyebrow.

"Glory?" I asked. "What about eating lunch with Glory?"

Isabella shook her head. "Glory brings her own food and likes to eat by herself and text to her boyfriend. That's why I'm so excited to see you here!" Isabella said. "I have someone to eat lunch with now."

I couldn't blame Isabella. I knew how hard it was at school to not have anyone to eat lunch or breakfast with. I usually hurried with lunch and went to the library, where a lot of the boys played games on the computer and I made notes in my science journal. It wouldn't hurt to have lunch with Isabella. It wasn't like we were at school, it was just one Saturday lunch. "What do you have in the bag?" I was kinda hungry.

Isabella reached into her bag and pulled out an orange and handed it to me. "Here you go."

"Thanks," I said as the black oystercatcher's cries pierced the air. Glory stood by the rope and frowned at a group of what looked like eighth or ninth grade boys. "I better get back to the black oystercatchers."

"I'll come with you!" Isabella tucked her bag into the back of the truck and rustled around in the bin for her name tag. She grabbed a silver counter from the box beside the name tag bin. "I've got the counter!"

"I think I should use the counter today," I said. I wanted to be sure and get the right number of people who we talked to for the data.

"I've got it." Isabella shifted on the thick sand. She lowered her voice. "I don't really want to volunteer with SEALS, but Mom thought it would be a good thing for me to do right now. My sister was friends with Glory. Before …" Isabella trailed off.

I knew there was more to Isabella's story than she was telling. Both Isabella and Max had stories that were not seen, just like the tides hide the sea stars. But so did Mom and I. Mom didn't want Aunt Charlotte to know too much about us. Mom had started calling Aunt Charlotte back on Sundays, and told her everything was going well, she didn't need any help and I was adjusting just fine. But she declined offers of dinner and said we were too busy with guests and running the cottages.

Isabella rubbed her stomach. "I don't feel good. I think I'll go sit in the truck for a while." She slipped the counter out of her pocket and gave it to me. "You count. I'll see you in a little while for lunch."

"Okay." I pocketed the counter. "I hope you feel better."

Isabella briefly nodded and climbed into the truck as I headed to the oystercatchers. Max and Honeybear had moved down the beach. Max walked in long steps while Honeybear trotted beside him on leash A couple at the tide pools talked to Martina and Angelina. Isabella said Martina and Angelina only liked to eat lunch together, and Martina only wanted to be friends with Sofia at school. Martina had unseen stories too.

10

SEA STAR SURVEY

On Wednesday, Mr. Carson gathered us into the morning meeting and flipped the class schedule to Clubs Day. Everyone cheered and I yelled just as loud. Mr. Carson told us to use our inside voices, but he was smiling so we knew it was okay to be excited about Clubs Day. I couldn't wait to show Autumn and Devon the sea star data collecting sheet. Clubs met every two weeks, so it had given me a lot of time to practice setting up a sea star spreadsheet for our trip to the beach to count them. I created rows and columns with space for a current count, sizes of each, and the location. I marked a picture of Sea Rock into four sections and labeled each of the quadrants with a number that corresponded with the chart. According to my research, most of the sea stars were in the left bottom quadrant. I couldn't wait to go to the beach with Autumn and Devon and count the sea stars today!

At 2:00 p.m., Mr. Carson finally told us to pack it up and head to our clubs meeting areas. I was the first person out of the classroom. I ran up the ramp to the portable and threw open the door. Devon sat at a small circular table and worked on his laptop. His wheelchair made him tall and his knees hit the bottom of the table. There weren't any chairs placed around the table, so I grabbed one from a small stack of four leaning against the back wall.

"What are you doing?" I leaned on my elbows and peered at his screen.

"Editing pictures that I took last night of my family." He didn't take his eyes off the screen. It looked like he was using a photo program to adjust the coloring of each person in each photo. Another screen was open to a chat box. In the box, conversations about using the photo program moved as people posted. Occasionally, Devon typed a quick emoji or comment in response to something in the chat box.

In Devon's photo, Kyra and her parents gathered around a table with a board game that looked like Monopoly. A fireplace glowed in the background and small lamps lit the room. I couldn't remember the last time Mom and I played a game together. Mom was taking online business classes at the community college and worked late into the night. Sometimes I found a *National Geographic* movie to watch on TV. Other times I worked in my room on my science experiments. I knew Mom's classes were important to her. But sometimes I wished she had more time to play a game with me. My chest felt funny and I turned away from Devon's pictures.

Devon didn't take his eyes from his screen but said, "We don't really have a fireplace. We used to, but we moved to a house without stairs and there isn't a fireplace in our house now."

I looked back at the photo. Could Devon insert me into that photo, too, like he did with the fireplace? I would like to be a part of his family game night. Kyra had been on the beach the last couple of Saturdays, but she was very serious. Unlike Glory, who talked to me, or Angelina, who spent time with

Martina, Kyra kept to herself and managed the adult volunteers. There were usually two adult volunteers for every SEALS shift and they seemed to really enjoy talking to the guests and answering questions.

Kyra also managed the social media accounts for SEALS and often spent time taking pictures and uploading funny sayings and quotes about the pictures on the social media accounts. I thought it was interesting how she could be so quiet on the beach, but so lively and animated when she posted pictures and quotes. It would be fun to have her as an older sister.

A horn beeped outside the portable and I ran to the door that I had forgotten to shut. "It's Autumn! We're going to the beach today!"

Devon didn't raise his head. "Have fun."

"Come on!" I danced around him. "We're going to do the sea star survey."

Devon kept working on his photo editing. He ducked his head and typed fast and hard in the chat box.

"What are you doing?" I asked.

"I'm not going to the beach. These are my friends," he waved his hand over the chat box.

"Those are your friends?" I looked at the box where a bunch of comments about how to draw an item in a photo filled the box. "How can those be your friends?"

Devon shrugged. "I have a lot of friends online. I don't want to go to the beach. I want to talk to my friends."

"But we need you to take pictures of the sea stars," I said. "Photograph the research just like you said." I didn't understand why Devon didn't want to go to the beach. He had been so excited last time to help with the sea star project.

"You take pictures." Devon reached into his bag and pulled

out his camera. He set it on the table. "I can't go to the beach. The wheelchair doesn't go over the sand."

"Oh." I stared at the wheels on Devon's chair. Devon couldn't travel over the beach like me. His wheels would get stuck in the thick heavy sand. "We can do something else," I said. "Something we both can do."

I smiled at him. The sea star survey could wait. I could take pictures and gather data and then bring it all to Devon so we could work on it together. It was more important that we do something together.

Autumn pushed open the door. "Come on, you two. It's beach day." Today she wore black leggings, tall red wading boots, a long red sweater that dropped almost to the wading boots and a yellow and red scarf. Her hair was in braids and as she moved her head, they swung back and forth. Her SEALS name badge was clipped to the side of her sweater as well as her badge saying she was the director of the program.

"We don't want to go." I dropped into a chair in front of Devon. "It's raining."

"What?" Autumn eyed me. "You've been talking about the sea star survey for the last two weeks with the SEALS. Glory said you can't stop talking about it!" She looked out the window. "It's not raining at all. It's a beautiful sunny day! It's a minus tide at the perfect time for our club today. We'll really be able to get out to count the sea stars as they're uncovered by the tide."

I lowered my head and motioned for Autumn to lean closer. "Devon's wheelchair can't go in the sand," I whispered.

"I reserved one of the beach wheelchairs," Autumn said in her regular voice. "We'll stop at the city hall and pick it up."

"Beach wheelchairs?" Devon lifted his head from his photos.

"The chairs have super big wheels that are made for the

sand," Autumn said. "The SEALS program just got a special grant for them. People love them!"

"Let's go!" Devon slapped his computer screen closed. "What are you two waiting for?" He wheeled himself to the door and grinned at us.

"Let's go!" I hoisted my backpack onto my shoulder and danced out the door. I was glad Devon had forgotten all about his online friends.

On the car ride to the beach, Autumn entertained us with funny stories about school field trips and what happened when kids had to go to the bathroom and realized the restrooms were a quarter mile up the beach. She told us about the lifeguard "bathroom," a small, secluded space in the dunes that was mostly out of sight. The lifeguards kept a roll of toilet paper and a notebook in a small metal box tucked into the dunes, so you could log that you had been there. Last summer, they figured out word had gotten out about their makeshift bathroom when they noticed people logging in locations like California and Idaho. This year they were talking about moving it.

She said the lifeguards hadn't set up for the summer yet. In a few weeks, on Memorial Day weekend, they would set up the poles placed up and down the three-mile beach with a rope that triggered an alarm, so if someone was in trouble the lifeguards could reach them in their small carts or truck.

Autumn pulled into a space in the public parking lot in front of City Hall. She went inside to pick up the wheelchair. As we waited for her, I pointed across the street to the wrong puffin and suggested we might need a midnight painting excursion for the "A" in our STEAM club. Devon giggled and we were both laughing when Autumn appeared at the car with the wheelchair. The thick wheels made both of us laugh harder and Autumn said she felt a little left out of our exclusive club of jokes. But neither of us told her what was so funny. Some things were just not meant to be shared.

Once we stopped laughing, it didn't take long for Devon to hoist himself into the chair with a little help from Autumn. He gave the chair a spin around the parking lot and said it worked better than his regular one, except it wasn't electric like his chair so he didn't go as fast.

I checked my backpack to make sure we had a small flashlight and stuck the sea star spreadsheet on a clipboard Autumn handed me. The flashlight would help us see the baby sea stars for our count.

On the beach, I pushed Devon over the sand to the left side of Sea Rock.

The tide was way out in a minus tide. Autumn had been right, it was perfect for our survey. Devon shone the flashlight and I counted the sea stars, making sure not to touch them. Autumn recorded the information on the data sheet. We counted three sea stars, which seemed good to me since most of them didn't grow to maturity, and twenty-two baby stars.

Devon took pictures of the sea stars and a few pictures of us as we collected the data. In one of the pictures, I stuck out my tongue and made funny eyes at his camera. He laughed and said he was going to include that picture in our research too.

We finished the count and I said I would come back in a couple of weeks and take another count to see how it had changed. Then we could compare the two sets of data. I hoped to do it all summer, and by the fall have a set count for the sea stars at Sea Rock so we could submit it to the scientists who were trying to track the sea stars up and down the entire coast from Washington State to California. Autumn reminded me that the tide wouldn't be a minus tide again for another few weeks and to be careful because there were small rip tides around Sea Rock that could easily catch me off guard and knock me over. I promised her I would be very careful.

After we finished the sea star survey, Autumn let us explore the tide pools. She pointed out nudibranchs and sea slugs. Devon took lots of pictures and I did a couple of drawings in my journal. When I got hungry, I opened my pack and pulled out the granola bar I had saved from lunch.

"Do you want some?" I offered half to Devon.

Devon took it and peeled off the wrapper. "I wish I wasn't in this chair." Devon took a bite of his granola bar. He chewed. "Sometimes I just wish I could play soccer again." Devon didn't look at me, as if he was embarrassed he had just told me too much.

I chewed on my granola bar. The cool air blew across my cheeks. I didn't want a friend who could run and play soccer. I wanted a friend who could help with the sea star survey and who was smart about science.

"I hate soccer." The granola got stuck in the back of my mouth and I wished I had water with me. "But I like science." I choked over the granola.

Devon unscrewed his water bottle cap and handed it to me. He hadn't taken a drink yet and I gulped half the bottle. "The doctors say I won't walk again, but Dad says we might go to some special doctors in Texas."

"I hope the special doctor can help you walk again." I wanted to tell Devon something about me too. Something important. "My dad grew up in Sea Rock Cove." I rolled the water bottle cap back and forth in my palm. "Aunt Charlotte still lives here. She was Dad's sister, but he didn't like her very much. Mom and I don't really talk to her." I paused. "Dad said my grandfather died, but Thomas said he's still living. I think Thomas is right. I think my grandpa is still in Sea Rock Cove somewhere." The words flew out of my mouth. "But, I'm not sure if I want to find out who it is." I exhaled.

"You've got to find out," Devon said. "Don't you want to meet your grandpa?"

"Yes." I nodded. "No. I don't know." One part of me did want to meet Dad's dad and have a grandfather. It would be kinda like Dad was here again. But the other part of me didn't want to know him. There had to be a reason Dad had said he had died. What if my grandfather had done something really horrible? What if he didn't want a granddaughter?

Autumn stepped up beside us. "It's time to go. You two ready?" She peered at both of us. "Are you okay?"

Devon nodded and I hopped behind him to push the chair. "We were just talking." Autumn wasn't too much older than us, and I knew the SEALS talked about a lot of things together. But sometimes there were things you just didn't want to talk about with grown-ups. Sometimes you just wanted to talk to your, hopefully soon, best friend.

I leaned down and squeezed Devon's hand as I wheeled him toward the dunes. "If I decide to find out who my grandfather is," I whispered, "you will be the first to know."

Devon squeezed my hand back. "I will be there for you, Lucy."

My insides felt warm. Devon was my friend. A real friend.

11
BUNNIES

*M*om double-checked the time of the city council meeting on her cell phone and dropped it back into her black bag. She wore her favorite turquoise scoop-neck top with a light blue scarf and jeans. Small hoop earrings dangled from her ears and she dabbed on a light pink lipstick. It had taken Mom about a month to decide she needed to do something about the bunnies. There had been too many close calls with guests and their dogs in the last few weeks. A quick check of the agenda for the mid-May city council meeting had made her resolve to address the issue.

Mom convinced me that I should wear my best blue jeans and a purple sweater that fit me correctly in the arms, and pull my hair into a scrunchie away from my face. She wanted me to wear my nice loafers, too, but I wore my knee-high boots. They had colorful swirls and designs in pink, purple and gold on the outside. A few nights ago, Glory had stopped by with the boots. She said she didn't wear them anymore and liked her boots with warmer material inside. They had almost fit and I stuffed socks into the toes so my feet slid up against the socks and the boots didn't fall off. I hadn't taken them off since.

"It'll be okay, Mom," I reassured her as we drove the five blocks to City Hall. "No one is going to be upset when you tell them why the bunnies are a problem. You manage a rental business. They have to understand that."

"I don't know." Mom shook her head and a strand of hair slipped out of her barrette and across her forehead. She pulled into a parking space in front of the long, one-story rectangular building. The back part of the building was where the police were located and where they parked their cars. The SEALS parked their truck there, as well. The front part of the building had the big room used for the big council meetings. "The Friends of the Bunnies have plastered signs all over town about tonight's city council meeting. They don't think the bunnies are a problem."

For the last week, I had seen the signs everywhere. Cute pictures of bunnies eating grass with "Don't Kill the Bunnies" printed at the top of the flyers. Apparently, a homeowner who had an infestation of bunnies under her house got tired of the city not doing anything to get rid of them. She wanted to take things into her own hands and remove the bunnies by packing them up into cages and releasing them somewhere else. The problem was, they were domesticated bunnies, not rabbits. They couldn't just be hauled into cages and released into the wild. They depended on the tourists and some locals feeding them, and eating in the local gardens. The Friends of the Bunnies wanted the city council to rule on an ordinance which protected the bunnies from homeowners who wanted to poison or relocated them, which wasn't a bad idea, but Mom was sick of the bunnies and too many close calls with dogs. She hung up small signs in each cottage about not feeding the bunnies, hoping that would at least send them to other places in the town. But we had both caught more than one guest with a carrot in their hands and a bunny munching happily.

Rain tapped on our roof. Even though Memorial Day was only a few weeks away and summer should have started, the rain kept coming. There had been a couple of Saturdays at SEALS where we all ended up sitting in the warm SEALS truck. There weren't that many people on the beach, but we had to stay on shift even during the rain, so we all got into the truck. The older SEALS girls always sat in the front of the cab. Isabella, Martina and I sat in the back seat and listened to Angelina and Glory and sometimes Kyra talk about dating and what they wanted to do with their lives.

Glory wanted to go to Australia and publish a woman's surfing magazine. She said surfing was all about men and she wanted to showcase women's surfing. Angelina's boyfriend studied at Portland State University. She told us all about the great food in Portland and how they wanted to open a restaurant together one day. Kyra had been at University of Washington and wanted to work in genetics, but when Devon had his accident she came home and took a job as volunteer coordinator at Sea Rock to help out with expenses. She talked about how sometimes you had to pivot and just be okay with how things went. She always seemed the oldest and wisest of all the SEALS girls.

Mom and I hurried into the brightly lit building. People stood everywhere inside the chamber hall. I recognized Angelina and Kyra standing against the back wall right away and waved to them. Aunt Charlotte stood near them and talked to two women who helped at the food closet. She waved at us, but Mom headed toward the middle of the room. Chairs had been set out in rows and almost all of them were filled. A tall pot of coffee was on the back table with a plate of cookies, but no one ate them. I slipped to the table and grabbed a double chocolate chip cookie from the tray.

Mom motioned me to two seats in the middle of the room. I squeezed past a row of Friends of the Bunnies people wearing bunny shirts and sat down between Martina and Mom. A man who looked a lot like Martina sat on her right side. Both wore Friends of the Bunnies t-shirts.

Martina held a stack of papers on her lap. The top sheet was a speech and below, a stack of Friends of the Bunnies flyers.

"I hope you're here to support the bunnies," Martina said to me.

Before I could answer, a man at a round table, with a small sign in front of him that said Mayor Simmons, tapped a gravel. The room silenced and people sat down. There were six people at the table. Each of them had a name plate in front of them saying Councilor.

A woman sat on the left side of the room by the door and checked people in on a clipboard as they signed up to speak. Officer Fredricks sat next to her. Did council meetings need a police officer to keep the peace when it was about bunnies?

"Good evening," Mayor Simmons said. "I think we all know why everyone is here tonight. Before we get started, I would like to remind everyone to speak with civility. Each person will have five minutes to speak. There is no booing or jeering allowed."

I shifted on the hard chair. The mayor seemed like a school principal reminding us of the rules before a guest speaker in the auditorium.

For the next hour, people filed up to the microphone. They gave their city and name before they talked. Some were from towns along the coast, a couple were from Sea Rock Cove, but a lot were from Portland and some from Seattle. They all passionately declared their love for the bunnies. No one spoke against the bunnies.

At the break, Mom whispered to me. "I don't think I'm going to talk."

"What? That's why we came!" I said.

"I know." Mom cleared her throat. "But I didn't realize this many people were going to be for the bunnies. I don't want to lose business."

"I am going to talk for us!" I threaded my way to the signup clipboard and signed my name on the list.

After people had a chance to eat some of the cookies and drink the coffee, the mayor called the room back to order. It didn't take long for my turn to talk to come up. My legs didn't shake at all on the way to the podium, but my stomach moved around like something from the tide pools was inside making me a little queasy.

At the podium, Officer Fredricks adjusted the microphone lower for me.

"Hello," I said. "My name is Lucy Lavender." My voice seemed to echo in the room. "My mom," I motioned toward Mom and her face turned red. "She manages the Villas at Sea Rock Cove. The bunnies are a problem. People who bring dogs can't stop the dogs from chasing the bunnies. One dog almost got hit by a car!"

The room stilled. The people of Sea Rock Cove loved dogs more than bunnies.

"We don't want the bunnies to be harmed, and poisoning is wrong, but something must be done. There are too many of them." From behind me, there were a few cheers and claps.

I remembered to say thank you and returned to my seat. Mom smiled at me and patted my leg. She leaned over and whispered in my ear, "Good job."

Martina shifted away from me, and I didn't look at her.

After my speech, more people talked about the damage from the bunnies. The bunnies got under houses and made homes there. They ate up landscape and gardens. It wasn't just one bunny. There were too many bunnies everywhere.

I was pretty sure people against the bunnies were making a very good case. The Friends of the Bunnies shifted in their seats, cleared their throats, and pulled out cell phones.

And then Martina stood up to speak. She walked to the podium and the room silenced. "Hello," she said. "My name is Martina Gonzola. I live with my uncle. My parents were taken away while I was at school." She swallowed and stared down at her paper. There wasn't one cough or movement in a chair from anyone.

I studied Martina and pictured the sea stars being uncovered at low tide. Their purple and orange arms holding onto the rock and mussels. Martina was like those sea stars right now as she shared her unseen story.

"I was very sad and upset about my parents," Martina continued in her soft voice. "I worry about my parents a lot and I don't trust a lot of people, but when I see the bunnies, I feel happy. Please don't get rid of the bunnies."

Martina turned from the podium and quickly walked to her seat. She didn't look at anyone. Her uncle stared straight ahead at the councilors.

I fiddled with the corners of the Friends of the Bunnies paper. What would it be like if I came home one day to find Mom gone, with no way to find out what happened to her? My stomach clenched. I couldn't imagine how it would be without Mom. My closest relative was Aunt Charlotte and I would not want to live with Aunt Charlotte.

No one else stood up to talk.

"Thank you to all who spoke," Mayor Simmons said. "The

council will discuss all that we have heard tonight and make a ruling in two weeks."

Everyone in the room stood. Before I could say anything to Martina, a crowd of people surrounded her. They complimented her for her bravery.

Mom tapped me on the shoulder. "Want to go get pizza? A guest left a coupon for us that they couldn't use." She smiled at me. Mom and I loved when guests left coupons or discounts for local restaurants. It was a treat to go out to dinner.

I slipped into my coat and headed out the door with Mom. I didn't say much on the drive to the pizza restaurant. I thought I had been right about the bunnies, but Martina's story made me realize there were always two sides to everything. Martina didn't see the bunnies as a problem like Mom and I did. She saw them as something which helped her.

* * *

THE PIZZA RESTAURANT wasn't big like the ones in some of the other places where we had lived, but the chairs had big cushions and I found an open table at the back by the kitchen.

I sank into a seat. We didn't need a menu. Mom didn't like a lot on her pizza and we always had pepperoni.

"You're quiet," Mom said after we placed our order.

"Just thinking." I took a swallow of my ice water. The ice bumped against my teeth.

"You did great up there tonight. I was so proud of you."

I chewed on my ice as the front door to the restaurant opened and people streamed into the pizza shop. Most of them had been at the city council meeting. Some stopped to talk to Mom and others didn't look at us.

The restaurant had gotten pretty crowded by the time Martina and her uncle stood in the doorway. A couple of people waved at them but no one had an empty seat at their table except Mom and me.

"Can we ask them to sit with us?" I asked. "We have room."

"Of course." Mom moved her purse and dropped it to the floor. "I want to talk to Isaac about doing some work around the cottages. A couple people have recommended him for some yard work." She pulled out the chair next to her and waved at Martina's uncle.

When they reached us, I looked directly at Martina and said. "Do you want to share a table with us?"

"Sure." Martina shrugged. She sank into the chair next to me and Uncle Isaac sat next to Mom.

It didn't take Martina and Uncle Isaac long to decide on a large sausage pizza with extra cheese. After they ordered, Uncle Isaac entertained us with funny stories. Mom turned pink-eared a couple of times. I eyed his left hand. He didn't wear a ring and neither did Mom. It had taken her a year to take off her ring after Dad died, but one day I noticed she wasn't wearing it anymore. I didn't say anything, but something in me shifted. I wished she still wore that ring.

When our pizza arrived, Mom and Uncle Isaac moved on to talk about the grounds around the cottages. I was glad to see her ears had returned to normal color and he wasn't telling funny stories only to her.

Martina and I talked about school. We both hated our music class with Mrs. Wilcox, who was so strict. We both loved volleyball days in PE. Martina said she might try out for the junior high school volleyball team next year. I thought that would be fun too. We didn't talk about the bunnies at all.

When we were finished, I stuck the leftover pizza in a small box. Uncle Isaac and Martina finished their pizza. But it took Mom and Uncle Isaac a long time to want to leave. Mom kept giggling and he kept telling more stories. Martina rolled her eyes at me and said loudly, "Uncle Isaac. I have homework to do." That stopped the conversation. But when Mom reached for her purse, Uncle Isaac tapped her hand and said, "I've got this." Mom blushed bright red but she let him pay for our pizza without the coupon.

When we got outside, Uncle Isaac shook Mom's hand for what seemed like a minute too much before he said goodbye. He and Martina slipped into a big white truck parked alongside the pizza shop.

In the far corner of the pizza shop patio, Thomas sat at one of the small picnic tables with Luna by his feet. He lifted his head to smile at me. The light wasn't good outside the pizza shop, but the color of his skin looked kinda grey.

"Are you okay?" I rushed to him.

"Yeah," Thomas nodded. "I'm just a little hungry. I didn't get anything to eat today."

"Here." I gave him the leftover pizza. I knew Mom wouldn't mind. She knew what it was like to be hungry. We both did.

"Thanks." Thomas tipped his head to me. "I appreciate it." He opened the box and broke off a chunk for Luna and then took a bite himself.

I hurried to the parking lot and caught up with Mom at the car.

"That was nice of you," Mom said as she opened the door.

I slipped inside and snapped on my belt buckle. "Do you think Thomas could live in one of our cottages sometimes? When no one is staying there."

Mom started the car and pulled out of the parking lot. She turned on her lights. Her windshield wipers swooshed back and forth. "I don't think that is a good idea. I'm sorry, hon. We need the cottages to be open for the guests, and it wouldn't make sense for Thomas to move in and out of them every time new guests arrive."

I peered out the window. Empty dark cottages lined the streets. Why wasn't there a home for Thomas if these homes were often empty? The bunnies reminded me there were always two sides to a story. Thomas and Luna had a story too, an unseen story.

12

COMMON MURRES

*O*n Saturday, I biked down Main Street where people filled the sidewalks, browsing in the small shops, eating late breakfasts on the restaurant patios. I didn't see Thomas playing his guitar, but the Bow Wow Beach Dog shop was busy and people and dogs filed in and out the doors. American flags flew from poles and buildings along Main Street, celebrating the Memorial Day weekend. As I biked past the crooked art gallery, Max stood on his deck, painting a landscape picture of the ocean, while Honeybear lay by his side, chewing on a raw bone. I waved and he nodded to me. A couple of people stood on the sidewalk and watched as he painted.

When I reached the center of town, I veered left and parked my bike in a set of racks along the back of the bookstore and a restaurant that smelled like bacon and eggs and pancakes. My stomach rumbled. Mom hadn't let me eat any of the pastries for the guests this morning and instead I'd had a bowl of cold cereal, which never filled me. I hoped one of the SEALS volunteers had brought food for us. Usually, there was at least one volunteer who handed out granola bars, home-made muffins and juice boxes.

I walked through the pathway leading to the beach and over the grassy dunes. On the beach, people were setting up their spots for the day. Tents with open fronts faced the ocean and clusters of families gathered inside with coolers of food. Children ran up and down the beach with buckets and shovels. People said summer in the Pacific Northwest didn't start until after the Fourth of July because of the rain, but by the looks of things, summer had arrived this weekend, which was a good thing for the Memorial Day crowds.

For the last two weeks, the cottages had been filled with a steady stream of guests both on the weekends and weekdays. Uncle Isaac worked on the lawn every day. He carved paths and trails, laid bark and brought Mom flowers. Mom said he had a lot to do. I didn't think he had *that* much to do. At school, Martina and I talked about it and agreed that Uncle Isaac was spending a little too much time with Mom.

The lifeguards had set up their poles along the three-mile beach and one or two drove in carts up and down the beach, making sure everyone was safe. A couple of lifeguards hung around the tall lifeguard stand near Sea Rock. It was hard not to miss Angelina talking to a very tall, dark-haired boy. She leaned against the white look-out stand and her laughter carried across the sand, filled with joy, flirtation and the promise of summer romance.

I wasn't ready for my own summer romance, but I was enjoying the chats Devon and I shared on our computers in the evenings. Mom let me use the cottage work computer to talk to Devon. We talked about our sea star research and the idea of having a BioBlitz to get people involved with the fate of the sea stars. I'd read about BioBlitzes online. People gathered data and recorded it in special apps. They logged it into the name of the BioBlitz project on the app and you could see all the different species people identified in a specific time and place. A BioBlitz was a good way to track data on lots of different species to study them over a period of time, and to track if a species was declining or increasing. It was great to have a friend who was interested in the same things as me.

During SEALS Saturdays, Martina had warmed up a little to me since the night we had pizza, but at school, Martina and Sofia still seemed pretty intent on keeping their shared secrets private by talking in Spanish whenever I could overhear them and Mr. Carson wasn't monitoring us. I was glad school would be out in another week. I planned to spend a lot more time volunteering with SEALS and helping Mom at the cottages. Maybe if I helped her more, Uncle Isaac would help her less.

When I reached Sea Rock, a swarm of people surrounded the SEALS truck, looking at the art panels, reading the brochures we kept in plastic racks and asking questions. The volunteers wore short-sleeve shirts and blue caps with the SEALS emblem stitched on the bill. No one wore their rain jackets today.

Glory sat behind a long folding table that had been placed facing Sea Rock. A stack of coloring pages were under her left arm. Open packs of watercolors lay on the table. A family with two children stood in front of Glory as she explained that the small black and white birds, which sometimes people thought were little penguins, were actually common murres. The common murre laid one pear-shaped egg a season. It took one hundred days to hatch—the longest incubation period of all the birds. It would be mid-fall by the time all the fledglings left Sea Rock.

"Have a seat." Glory waved at the extra chair next to her. "I could use a second pair of hands. We are swamped with all the visitors for the Memorial Day weekend."

I stepped behind the table and slid into the folding chair next to Glory. I didn't mention the fact that Angelina wasn't at the tide pools, she was flirting with the lifeguards behind us. Martina stood by herself at the tide pools. Kyra stood at the base of Sea Rock beside the rope which protected the black oystercatchers' nest. Autumn led a group of people on a private tour, and I didn't see Isabella anywhere, which I thought was odd because it was Memorial Day weekend and it seemed like everyone who owned a second home at Sea Rock Cove was here.

Glory handed me a bird coloring page. I dipped a brush into the black watercolor paint as the sun beat down on my head.

"You need a hat!" One of the adult volunteers who always brought breakfast bars and juices for everyone on her shift, placed a SEALS cap on my head. "Don't let your face get burned." She handed me a bottle of suntan lotion with extra protection. I didn't see any sign of the juice boxes or granola bars today.

I set my brush down and lathered the suntan lotion across my cheeks and forehead as a little girl who looked to be about five or six, with curly blond hair, stood in front of me. She wore a red t-shirt that said Sea Rock Cove and had a picture of a puffin across the front. It was one the SEALS sold to raise money for the Pacific tufted puffin research, so they could learn more about what the birds did from mid-August to April, when they flew out to sea and weren't nesting on Sea Rock.

"I'm making my picture for my dad." The girl pulled one of the paint sets closer. "Is your picture for your dad, too?"

"I don't have a dad." I swallowed hard. Dad had been gone

for three years this weekend. Usually Mom and I did something special mark the day. The first year, Mom and I went to a park with a big area for dogs. We watched all the dogs playing and it took away that achy feeling inside. The second year, she got special tickets to the Museum of Science and we had lunch afterwards in the museum café. This year, Mom had been too busy with the cottages and she hadn't said anything about doing something special.

"Did you know the common murres are the best fathers in the bird kingdom?" Glory said to the girl.

"I have the best dad." The girl painted her bird picture and the watercolors ran outside the lines.

"I'm sure you do," Glory said and continued with her speech. "After the chick hatches, the mother murre goes back to the ocean and leaves the father to help the chick learn to swim and feed."

Glory talked a lot about her dad. She didn't see him much because he lived in California, but he had taught her to surf. She said whenever she went out surfing, she always felt close to him.

I fingered my sea star necklace and made sure it lay outside my shirt and not inside.

A tall thin man standing next to the little girl picked up one of the three spotted eggs sitting on the table. "What are these markings?"

"Those are how the common murres tell which egg belongs to them. Each egg is marked differently so they can identify it," Glory continued in her same singsong voice. Did she ever get tired of saying the same thing over and over? Glory had been working for SEALS for three summers. She said this was her last one and after this she was going to Australia. She had just about enough money saved up to get her there.

The little girl leaned across the table. "I can share my dad with you," she whispered in a not so quiet voice.

"That's okay." I picked up my brush and moved it in straight lines and ran the facts about common murres over in my head like something I needed to memorize for school. The thing about science was, everything could be explained with numbers and data. It wasn't confusing like all the feelings inside of me now. Sometimes I felt angry that Dad was gone and other times sad. I never knew which one it was going to be. Today a mix of both swirled inside me.

"Zoey." The tall thin man placed his hand on the girl's shoulders. "Come on, let's give someone else room at the table. I want to check out the sea stars and the tide pools."

"The sea stars are gone," I said, without looking up.

"Gone?" the man asked.

"They have a disease." My insides twisted and I enjoyed this moment of telling this man and his daughter that the sea stars were dying. It somehow made me feel better to tell them something hurtful and pass along some of the injustice I felt about losing Dad. "They're dying. Everything dies."

Glory cleared her throat and stared at me.

"Everything dies," I said, ignoring Glory. "It's part of the life cycle. No use pretending otherwise."

"What she means," Glory said, interrupting me. "Is that the sea stars have a virus that started infecting them a few years ago. However," she looked at me, "you can still see some at Sea Rock. They are usually on the left side."

I didn't look at Glory. I had just broken the number one rule at SEALS: Be positive and friendly to the guests.

"Thank you." The man tapped his daughter on her head. She stood and handed him the picture she had painted. He hugged her and the two walked toward Sea Rock holding hands. The feeling inside of me intensified and I painted hard black lines across my common murre. I was ruining the picture, but I didn't care. All I could feel was the darkness around me.

"That was rude," Glory said. "What's going on with you? You love the sea stars."

"Nothing," I muttered. I didn't want to talk to Glory about how I felt. She wouldn't understand. She had a dad.

Glory shook her head. "Okay. If you don't want to talk to me, please take off your SEALS hat. Your shift is over."

I knew I could talk to Glory. I could tell her everything. I could tell her about Dad and how he died. I could tell her about the sea stars and why it was important to Dad. I could tell her how Uncle Isaac was spending a lot of time at our house and I didn't want him to become my new dad. I could talk to her about how Mom and I had struggled and we never had enough to eat and sometimes we had to sleep in our car for a while until Mom found a new job. But I didn't want pity from Glory. I looked up to Glory and I wanted her to see me as strong and smart.

I left my drawing on the table and dropped the SEALS hat beside it. The tears started falling as soon as I turned away from Glory and I headed up the beach toward home. I didn't feel strong and smart. I felt weak and ashamed.

13

SICK

On Sunday, Mom ran out of the morning pastries and asked if I could run up to the bakery to get a few scones. "Go to the side window," she said. "I'll text Vivian to let her know you're coming."

I hopped on my bike and whisked past the town bus stop shelter. It wasn't a busy bus shelter, not like the ones in the city. During the summer, a small bus drove from north to south and picked up people so they didn't have to clog up the small main street with their cars. Once a day, a bus arrived from Portland and dropped off people who came from there. The rest of the time it was empty.

A figure huddled in a dark blanket inside the bus shelter. Luna lay on the bench.

"Thomas?" I pressed hard on my bike brakes and jumped off. The bike crashed to the ground. I stepped into the bus shelter and covered my mouth. It smelled bad. Really bad. Like throw-up and something else I couldn't quite name.

Thomas let out a groan from under the blanket. Luna looked at me with sad, pleading eyes.

"Thomas are you sick?" I didn't want to get much closer. The smell made me gag.

Thomas groaned again.

The scones didn't matter. I had to get help for Thomas. The police station was located behind City Hall which was just steps from the bus shelter.

"I'll be right back." I hopped on my bike and pedaled as fast as I could.

The thick blue door of the police station was closed when I arrived. But a small window opened and a woman in a police uniform asked, "Can I help you?"

"There is a sick man," I said. "At the bus shelter. Can you help him?"

Officer Fredricks pushed open the heavy blue door. He stood in the doorway. "Thomas?"

"Yes," I said. "Please help. He's really sick."

Officer Fredrick hustled with me back to the bus shelter and stepped inside. He knelt beside Thomas. "Thomas? Can we help you?" He placed his hand on the blanket.

Thomas groaned.

Officer Fredricks spoke into his walkie-talkie. "We need an aid car at the bus stop."

He pocketed his walkie-talkie. "Help is on the way. We'll get him up to the hospital in Pelican Shores."

"What about Luna?" I asked. "Where will she go?"

Officer Fredricks eyed me. "Do you want to watch her for a little while? We can keep her in the police station, but I think she might enjoy being with you, if you can do it."

"Yes," I said without thinking twice. Mom wouldn't mind. We allowed dogs in the cottages. I would just use the side yard like the cottage guests and pick up her poops with the blue bags. "Luna and I are good friends. I'll take her to the Bow Wow pet shop and get a treat for her." I petted

Luna's back. She nestled closer to me and leaned in against my leg.

"That would be perfect," Officer Fredricks said and smiled at me. "I'm sure she would like to be with you. Stop by the station and pick up some dog food. We have some for our K-9, Asher, and would be happy to share with Luna."

The aid car pulled around the corner from the fire station, which was just two blocks away. Even though we didn't have a hospital in Sea Rock Cove, we did have a fire station with one aid car and two fire trucks. The sirens to the aid car were off. I guessed it was because they weren't coming from that far away.

The medics loaded Thomas onto a stretcher and into the back and prepared to transport him to the hospital in Pelican Shores. I walked Luna to the side of the shelter and stood with her. She whined a little but stayed out of the way.

"I'll check in with you," Officer Fredricks said. "I've got to head out now to do my rounds. No school on Monday for Memorial Day, so I'm guessing you'll be out with SEALS tomorrow? I hear you are doing great work."

I flushed. I didn't want to tell him I had acted so badly yesterday that I wasn't even sure Glory wanted me to go back to SEALS. "Yes," I mumbled.

When we got home, Mom met me at the door. She frowned. "What are you doing with a dog? Where are the scones?"

"It's Thomas's dog," I said. "He's sick and had to go to the hospital. I'm fostering her for a while. I couldn't go to the bakery because I couldn't juggle Luna and my bike and the crowds on Main Street."

Mom gave me the look. That one she gives me when she knows she's going to have to go along and doesn't like it one bit. "Okay," she said and sighed. "But you need to keep her away from the guests' dogs. And no matter what, be sure she does not get any of the bunnies!"

Mom swept her hair off her forehead. "Cottage number four has a young girl staying with her dad and she's been feeding the bunnies. I think she thinks they're her pets. They were at Sea Rock yesterday and she made him a cute picture of the black and white birds and put it up in their window." Mom smiled and looked at me. "What are the names of those black and white birds?"

"The common murres," I muttered. I didn't tell Mom I was pretty sure I knew who the young girl was and I had met her on the beach yesterday and didn't act so nice. The last thing I needed was for Luna to attack one of the bunnies the girl had adopted as a pet and was feeding!

For the rest of the day, I kept myself busy with Luna. I found an old tennis ball one of the guests had left in the side yard and threw it for her a few times. She didn't really seem to like playing catch and did a slow amble to get the ball and then didn't bring it back to me. I didn't let her go anywhere near the bunnies or cottage number four. I finally took her into my room and made a bed out of blankets and towels.

The next morning, I made sure to get up early and take Luna outside so she didn't make any messes on the floor.

When I came back inside, Mom said, "Don't you have a volunteer shift today? It's Memorial Day. They'll be busy at Sea Rock."

"Mmmmm …" I muttered. "I think so."

Mom studied me for a minute. "I'll keep Luna. You go to Sea Rock. I've got things under control here. Pretty much everyone has headed to the beach with coolers and chairs so I think it's going to be pretty quiet around here today. I'll work on some paperwork and Luna can sit inside with me."

"Okay." I grabbed my backpack by the door. Since

everyone seemed to think I should be at Sea Rock, I could at least go down to the beach. I didn't have to volunteer. I could just hang out at the beach for a while and catch up with my science journal notes. I wanted to do a special page showing all the different types of sea stars on the Oregon Coast. I had checked out a book from the library that had pictures of each of them. We only had a couple of species at Sea Rock, mainly the ochres. The wasting syndrome had attacked the sunflower sea star worst of all, and researchers were saying it might never come back.

Mom touched my shoulder. "Lucy?" she said softly. "I know this is the weekend you and I usually do something to honor your dad."

I nodded and my throat clogged with tears.

"It's really busy and I haven't been able to get away. But I promise, after school ends in another week or so, you and I will take a drive. We'll go to Seaman Point and explore. There's a maritime museum on the Columbia River. We'll poke around and see what we can find, okay?"

"That would be great." I hugged Mom in a hard embrace.

Luna nudged in between us and I stepped away from Mom as she wiped a tear from the corner of her left eye. "Have a good day," she said.

Mom stood with Luna at the door and I headed out, fighting back the wave of emotions cascading inside me.

When I reached the beach, the SEALS truck was spinning its wheels about fifty feet from Sea Rock. Huge clumps of sand flew everywhere. It looked like Glory had driven down the ramp and gotten stuck in the thick dry sand.

I ran to the truck. "What's going on?"

Glory leaned out the window. "We're stuck! The sand is too deep!"

She gunned the truck again and sand flew from behind. The truck didn't move.

"I'm calling Officer Fredricks." Autumn sat beside Glory in the front of the truck. She punched the non-emergency police number into her cell phone. "We're not getting this thing out of the sand without some help!"

Angelina and Martina sat in the back seat of the cab. They were organizing a pile of brochures into the plastic holders. Neither one seemed too upset by the stuck truck.

Glory gritted her teeth and pressed on the gas. "Everyone move at the same time. Jump." She laughed in a high pitch noise that I'd never heard from her before. Glory always seemed like she had everything under control.

Angelina, Martina and Autumn all popped up in their seats while I tried not to giggle. They all looked so silly trying to make the truck move. The wheels continued to spin as Glory pressed on the gas. Days of no rain had created a big sand pile-up and the wheels dug in hard.

An unmarked SUV accessed the beach from the ramp and pulled up beside us. Office Fredricks rolled down his window. "Glory," he said. "What's going on?"

"Sorry about this," Glory said as her face flushed. "The sand is a little deep and we got stuck."

"Let me see what I can do." Officer Fredricks parked the SUV away from the SEALS truck, where the sand was a little flatter and firmer, and stepped out. "I'll get behind the truck and give it a push and rock. You hold down the gas."

"I'm so sorry about this. I was running late and didn't pay attention to where I was driving. I drove right into the thick, deep part of the sand instead of staying on the wet, flat part," Glory continued to explain as her cheeks flushed bright red.

"It happens to all of us sometimes," Officer Fredricks said

and touched Glory's arm. "Don't worry. We'll get you out of here and on to your shift at Sea Rock."

Glory's shoulders dropped from their position up by her ears. She tucked a strand of hair behind her ear and nodded. "Thank you. I really appreciate it."

Office Fredricks walked to the back of the truck. "Ready?"

"Go!" Glory hollered out the open window. She gunned the gas pedal and the truck rocked but didn't move. The engine sputtered and died.

"I flooded it." Glory placed her head on the steering wheel. "This is going to take a while." Glory eyed the ocean. "We need to get out there. The tide is going out and I don't want people trampling all over the tide pools." She nodded to me. "Can you handle the left side with the sea stars while I work on this? Autumn has a private tour and Angelina and Martina can handle the tide pools."

I bit my lip. I had to say something to Glory about Saturday. I wanted her to think I was strong and capable, but sometimes strong and capable meant saying you were sorry. I liked how Glory had told Officer Fredricks that running late today had made her hurry and not pay attention to the sand build-up on the beach.

"Glory ..." I stopped. I could do this. It was okay to tell Glory about me. "I'm sorry about the other day. My dad died on Memorial Day weekend and Mom and I usually do something together. But this year she's so busy with the cottages she forgot. I got upset."

Glory nodded to me. "It's okay. We all get upset sometimes." She grimaced. "Today isn't my best hour either. But ..." Glory stared at me hard. "Just try to remember not to take it out on the guests, okay?"

"Okay." I danced a little jig and kicked sand around me. Glory wasn't mad at me. I wasn't banned from SEALS.

Autumn, Angelina and Martina gathered a few items from the back of the truck and headed toward Sea Rock.

I turned to Officer Fredricks. "Have you heard anything about Thomas?"

Officer Fredricks shook his head and peered out over the ocean. "He's sick, Lucy. He's very sick."

"What's wrong with him?" My heart pounded. Was Thomas going to die like Dad?

Office Fredricks sighed and then gave me that look adults do when they're ready to tell kids something that is going to be hard to hear. "He has an opiate addiction."

I knew enough about opiate addictions to know they weren't good. We had seen people with opiate addictions in some of the hotels where we stayed when we didn't have a place to live. They scared me and Mom usually made sure all our doors were locked tight and a piece of furniture shoved in front of the door.

But Thomas didn't seem like the people we had seen in the hotels. I knew Thomas. He loved to read and play his guitar and entertain people. He loved Luna.

"Can't someone help him?" I asked.

"It's tricky," Officer Fredricks said. "People who need help don't always take help. I've known him for a long time." He swallowed hard and looked out over the sea. "He's always been stubborn. We try to get him help and a place to live, but something always happens and he ends up back on the street."

Thomas and Luna *were* houseless and that's why Luna didn't have a dog tag with her address. She still should have one with a phone number. Maybe I could get her one and it could have the cottages' phone number on it, like I was her foster family. "Is he going to die?" I swallowed hard.

Officer Fredricks didn't say anything, and in that not saying anything, I knew the truth.

If Thomas didn't accept help, Thomas would die. But how did you help someone who didn't want to be helped?

* * *

WHEN I GOT to Sea Rock, the first thing I noticed was the absence of the high-pitched black oystercatchers. There were a handful of people gathered around the base of Sea Rock where the nest had been.

I ran toward the people. "Get away." I shooed them with my hands. "Get away!"

It didn't matter. The oystercatchers had been there on Saturday, but that was before I found Thomas sick in the bus stop. The egg was gone and so were the black oystercatcher parents. Thomas had been unable to do his job guarding them. With all the people on the beach during the Memorial Day weekend, the parents had been scared off by humans getting too close and the egg had been eaten by a predator.

It was just science, I told myself. Scientists couldn't get emotionally involved with their subjects. They had to collect the data. The black oystercatchers had made a nest in a place with a lot of human traffic. As much as we tried, we couldn't always stop human impact. Wasn't that what I told guests about the eagle when it swooped in for the common murres? But somehow this didn't seem the same. Things felt like they were crashing in. First Thomas and now the black oyster-catchers.

I headed toward the left side of the rock where a handful of purple and orange sea stars had been uncovered in the low tide. Coming toward me from the beach, Kyra pushed Devon in one of the special beach wheelchairs.

"Lucy!" Devon waved his arms in big windmill motions. "I'm going to help today!"

When they reached us, Devon held up his hand for a high five. "Kyra said it's really busy because of Memorial Day and SEALS needed help. We can tell people about the sea stars together!"

"Okay," I shrugged.

"What's wrong?" Devon eyed me. "Aren't you glad to see me?" His voice dropped and sounded sad. Immediately, I leaned over and tossed my arm across his shoulder in a sideways hug. "I am always glad to see you," I told him. It was true. There was no one I'd rather spend time with, talking about the sea stars at Sea Rock, than Devon.

"But what's wrong?" Devon shielded his eyes against the sun.

"The black oystercatchers are gone," I said. "Thomas is sick. The truck is stuck on the beach." I pointed toward the blue truck. "Everything is going wrong."

A couple of little kids jumped on the rocks in the tide pools and splashed into the water. They giggled and pushed each other. "Stop!" I yelled. I grabbed Devon's chair and wheeled him to the edge of the tide pools.

Martina and Angelina were surrounded by a group of people and were pointing at the tall cormorants positioned on the left side of Sea Rock. People congregated everywhere around Sea Rock, looking at the tide pools, pointing to the birds, standing at the base pointing out the sea stars. Most dogs were on leash, but a few were off and trampling into the tide pools. A couple of children poked at the green anemones in the tide pools. One lady dropped her coffee cup ring and it floated down the beach in the wind. She didn't go after it to pick it up.

The kids moved out of the tide pools and stuck their tongues out. Devon darted his tongue out of his mouth and licked the tip of his nose. I'd seen him do it at STEAM club and it always made me laugh. The kids stared at him. No one laughed. I wanted to stick my tongue out at the kids, but Glory would be really upset with me. I shook my head the way the older SEALS girls did when they were upset with a guest.

Today seemed like it was going to be one of those days that the wise SEALS girls always talked about happening at Sea Rock in the summer. A day where it was just one thing after another.

A small boy kneeled on a rock and stuck his finger inside a crevice.

"What are you doing?" I stepped up beside him.

"There's an octopus!" He continued to poke his finger inside the rock.

I was pretty sure there wasn't an octopus stuck in the rock crevice. Devon knew a lot about octopuses and told me everything he knew, and we didn't have them at Sea Rock. Sometimes fishing boats found octopuses when they went out to sea and brought them to the aquarium in Pelican Shores, but the octopuses didn't live long. The fishermen only brought in the larger, older octopuses. They left the smaller juveniles so they could have a longer life in the ocean.

"Come see the octopus! There's an octopus under the rock." A small cluster of people gathered around him.

I peered into the rock crevice. A long purple leg stuck out. If I didn't know the facts, it might look like an octopus.

"See." The boy grinned at me. "An octopus!"

"I think it's a sea star," I said. "A purple ochre. We are doing research on the sea stars." I pointed to Devon who half-way leaned out of his chair, trying to see inside the rock crevice.

"It's an octopus," the boy said. His voice firm and strong.

The common murres and puffins flew off the rock in small fluttering circles. They were busy nesting and gathering food for their young chicks. In mid-August, the puffins would go out to sea where they would stay until the spring when they would come back and nest again. They used the same burrows each year at Sea Rock, which I thought was pretty neat because that meant the young chicks born at Sea Rock would eventually return and raise their own nest of chicks. The only problem was, in the last few years, the numbers of tufted puffins were declining and fewer and fewer were returning to nest. No one had really done a study on where the puffins went when they were out to sea or what happened to them. I thought Devon and I should tackle getting to know more about the puffins after we finished the sea star research.

"I think you should tell everyone there's an octopus that lives under the rock," the boy said.

A small line had formed of people waiting to see the octopus. The way the sun hit the rocks it was impossible to tell if it really was an octopus or a sea star. And for today, I didn't mind. Because sometimes you just went along with things and made things up, and even though I was a scientist, sometimes stories made it seem a little more like everything could come out happily ever after. And somedays we all needed to believe in happily ever after, especially on days like today.

"Sure," I said. "It's an octopus."

"There's an octopus under the rock," I said to Devon.

"Sure there is." He stuck his tongue out at me and touched his nose.

I rolled my eyes and stuck out my tongue at him, making sure the Sea Rock guests weren't watching me.

Both of us giggled. I was glad Devon was at Sea Rock today. Having a friend made things that were hard, sad, or scary easier to deal with.

*M*om finished writing: "Do not feed the bunnies." A stack of construction paper signs lay on the coffee table. Each sign had a colorful picture of a bunny with a carrot. In the early June meeting, City Council ruled that there would be no feeding of wildlife, except for songbirds from feeders. Everyone knew the new ordinance was directed at the bunnies. But it seemed to me to be a good compromise. The bunnies wouldn't be trapped and removed, but they might not multiply as fast either.

"I'm taking Luna for a walk," I said to Mom.

"Have a nice time." She barely looked up from drawing a bunny foot in loopy line.

I clipped Luna's leash onto her collar. It had been a week since Thomas had been taken to the hospital in Pelican Shores. Officer Fredricks had called to tell me that it would be a while longer, and if Mom and I didn't mind, could we keep Luna for a little bit longer until Thomas was able to return?

I had been thrilled to keep Luna. Mom said she would watch Luna while I was at school. It was the last week of school and clubs had wrapped up. The ending of clubs didn't feel that sad since Devon and I would keep working on our sea star project during the summer, and I was going to volunteer with SEALS a lot more so I would still see Autumn.

We'd finally gotten to walk over to the junior high and take a tour, meet our seventh-grade teachers and hear about life in junior high from the eighth graders. Sofia and Martina both thought the eighth-grade boy who gave our tour was cute, and I was happy to see Devon join us and hear he would be attending junior high with us.

Luna adapted easily to our house. She didn't cry like puppies do on their first night in a new home when she slept in my room on the floor beside my bed. That first night, I had made her a big pile of my blankets and slept with only my sheet. Then I got a little cold and threw on a sweatshirt to sleep in. In the morning, when Mom woke me, she saw the sleeping arrangements. She brought in a stack of old blankets and sheets which had been removed from the cottages due to various stains or rips to use for Luna's new bed.

Now, I headed down our street and toward the pathway which led to the beach. Luna walked beside me and didn't pull on her leash at all. It was Friday afternoon and visitors were streaming into town for the first weekend of June. Schools had started to get out for the year and the rental cottages were filling up as families started their beach vacations.

When we got to the beach, I knew not to let her off her leash. Only dogs that had been trained to be under voice control and come when their owners called could be off leash. The beach wasn't as busy as Memorial Day weekend, but it was still busy. Dogs ran up and down the soft sand and I tried to keep her away from the off-leash dogs.

I made sure to walk very carefully through the families with children carrying sand buckets and parents carrying firewood and coolers of food. We passed a couple of people with dogs, but Luna never lunged toward any of them. When we got near the SEALS truck, Max stood beside the truck with a paintbrush.

"What are you doing?" I hadn't seen Max since the Saturday when I told him about Dad's sea stars and I'd spent a lot of time thinking about what Thomas had said about family. I stared hard at Max. Was he related to me? Was he family?

"Just a little touch-up," Max said. "The panels get a little beat up sometimes and I like to get out here and touch them up as the season really gets going." He nodded to Luna. "I see you got a dog. He looks familiar ..."

"Thomas's dog," I said. "He's sick. I'm taking care of Luna."

"I'm sorry to hear that." Max stopped painting and looked at me. "I've known him a long time. He's a good person who struggles."

I nodded. "I know about struggle. Mom and I struggle sometimes too."

Max's eyes widened and he frowned. "You do?"

"Yeah," I said. "Since my dad died, it's been hard for us." I stopped, pretty sure that I had said too much. Mom never wanted anyone to know we struggled, and especially not someone like Max who we barely knew.

"You tell your mom to come by the gallery," Max said firmly. "If you need anything. Anything at all."

"Okay," I said, quickly backtracking with Luna. Mom wouldn't like that I was talking about our problems to people who we didn't really know that well, and they were offering us help. "But we're good now. We have somewhere to live and Mom has a paycheck that buys us food and things."

"That's good," Max said, "But remember what I said. You need anything, I want you and your mom to be able to get some help. That's what we do at Sea Rock Cove. We help each other out."

I nodded and a warm feeling spread inside me. Mom and I had never lived in a town like Sea Rock Cove. We'd lived in a couple of small towns, but no one was as friendly and as helpful as they were at Sea Rock Cove. From Officer Fredricks who helped Thomas, to Martina and Angelina who helped at SEALS, to Max who offered to help Mom and me, it was like Sea Rock Cove was one big family. And maybe that's what Thomas had meant when he said it was good to know your family. Maybe it didn't have anything to do with blood relations and it was all about the family you made with the people around you.

I walked Luna away from Sea Rock and toward the quiet north end of the beach. Sea Rock Cove was divided into sections. The mid-section of town was where all the hotels were and where Mom and I lived. This was the section of the beach where Sea Rock was located, too. It was the busiest part of the three-mile beach. Most of the locals lived in the north and south ends of town. There weren't really that many locals who lived in Sea Rock Cove full-time, only about nine hundred people or so. But as the summer days began, it seemed like the town doubled in size because of all the people staying in their second homes and vacation rentals.

I walked near the large pieces of driftwood and picked up small pieces of microplastic. We had made a lot of pieces of jewelry from the microplastics in STEAM Club with Autumn. She said SEALS could sell them on their website and in some of the local stores and the money would go toward the SEALS program and things like research for the sea stars. My sea star necklace pressed against my neck where I always wore it. As much as I liked making the microplastic jewelry, I didn't really like wearing it. It felt a little clunky to me, and as Autumn said, it was more a conversation piece about beach trash than jewelry to wear every day. I slipped the microplastics into a blue dog poop bag. The SEALS had placed a box outside their office at City Hall where people could deposit beach trash.

Luna walked beside me. She was good on a leash, unlike some of the dogs I saw on the beach who tugged and pulled their owners. Sometimes Luna stopped at places where people had made campfires among the driftwood and sniffed extra hard.

At the farthest point of the north end of the beach, a surfer pulled on a wetsuit. I couldn't tell who it was, but I didn't think Glory usually surfed on this part of the beach. She liked to surf one of the State Park beaches about fifteen miles south of Sea Rock Cove. On the high tide line, a common murre sat on the sand. It was unusual to see common murres on the sand and not on Sea Rock. The bird tried to lift itself out of the sand and fly, but one of its wings leaned sideways and threw it off balance.

I walked Luna closer to the bird, but not too close. I wasn't sure if Luna had ever seen a common murre or what she might do with one. Especially one that was injured. But I needed to investigate. In order to get closer, I was going to have to set the leash on the sand and hope Luna stayed. I'd seen Luna sit beside Thomas while he played his guitar. She never moved. I hoped the same would work for me. "Stay Luna," I said in my best command voice. She looked at the bird and, as I had hoped, didn't move.

I crept closer to the injured bird. SEALS rescued birds. They kept crates, the kind for cats and dogs, in the back of the truck. We didn't have an animal carry cage at home, but I bet I could find a box and ask Mom to help me transport it to the aquarium. They took in injured sea life.

I bit my lower lip. But first I had to get the bird home and I wasn't sure how. I didn't have anything to wrap it in and I couldn't just carry it barehanded.

There were a couple of people scattered along the dunes, but most were couples snuggled together on blankets with picnics and I didn't want to interrupt them. I scanned the beach. My best bet was the surfer, who would probably have a sweatshirt or t-shirt to wrap the bird.

"Come on, girl." I grabbed Luna's leash and jogged up the beach to the surfer. Luna padded beside me and the wind ruffled her fur.

When I reached the surfer, I stopped.

Isabella wore wetsuit pants, but she hadn't zipped the top over her bathing suit yet. I hadn't seen her for a couple of weeks and no one had said why she wasn't there last weekend during Memorial Day. A thick sweatshirt lay beside her surfboard. I hoped she would let me wrap the injured common murre in her clothing.

"I need some help," I said to Isabella. "There's a bird. It has a hurt wing and I need a jacket to wrap it in." The words fell out of my mouth in a rush. After seeing how Isabella acted at SEALS, I wasn't sure if she would want to help. She never seemed to want to do too much with SEALS.

But Isabella scooped up her sweatshirt. "Where is the bird?

I pointed down the beach. "It's a common murre."

Isabella took off running so fast, Luna and I could barely keep up with her and her sweatshirt trailed out behind her like a kite in the wind. When she reached the bird, she quickly wrapped it in her sweatshirt. The bird's head peaked out through an opening she created from the sleeves.

"My mom transports birds to the Wildlife Rehabilitation Center in Seaman Point," Isabella said. "I help with some of the transports. I'll call her and tell her to meet us."

"What about surfing?"

"I'll text Glory. She was supposed to meet me. She's giving me lessons."

In a few minutes, Isabella had texted both Glory and her mom. I couldn't help but notice she had the latest cell phone and a fancy, colorful cover.

"You didn't come out for Memorial Day weekend?" I asked as we walked toward the dunes.

Isabella shook her head. Her face darkened. "We were waiting for some news and Mom and Dad didn't want to leave Seattle."

My mind whirled. What kind of news was Isabella's family waiting for? It didn't sound like good news, by the look on her face. I walked with Luna up the dunes, being careful to keep her away from Isabella and the bird. When we got to the top where the surfers usually parked, Isabella's mom was already waiting.

"She got here fast," I said.

"We live right over there." Isabella pointed to a three-story house that overlooked the ocean. A spacious deck encircled the home. I couldn't help it. A long whistle escaped my mouth.

"That's a big house for three people." I couldn't imagine what it would be like living in a house that big with just three people. And they didn't live here all the time either. They only came out some of the time and had another house in Seattle.

"There are four of us. I have an older sister," Isabella said, her voice softened. "She got angry with my parents and moved out. She doesn't talk to any of us, but sometimes we hear things from her friends and we think she might come home."

"That was the news you were waiting for?" I asked.

"Yes." Isabella nodded and hugged the bird a little closer to her chest. "We thought she might be coming home but she never showed up. Mom and Dad were pretty upset by Memorial Day night." She lowered her voice and it sounded as if tears were caught in her throat. "I was too. We thought this time it might be for real that she would come home."

"I'm sorry about your sister," I said. I couldn't imagine what that would be like, to always be waiting and wondering if someone you loved was going to come home, and if they were okay.

"It's why I volunteer with SEALS," Isabella continued. "My sister loved SEALS and spent all her time with them."

"But you don't like SEALS?" I asked.

Isabella shook her head. "SEALS belonged to my sister. I do it because it makes my parents happy, but it's not mine." She nodded to the ocean. "I love to surf. I want to move to Hawaii and compete in surfing competitions one day."

As much as I didn't like Isabella at SEALS, she seemed different now. As if the wind softened her and made her strong at the same time.

Isabella's mom opened the passenger door and pulled out a blue cat carry cage. Isabella opened the top and slipped the common murre inside and closed the cage again. Her mom placed the crate in the back seat.

"Do you want to come with us?" Isabella asked.

I shook my head. "I don't know if Luna will travel in a car. I'm watching her for a friend."

"Thomas?"

"Yes," I said. "How do you know Thomas?"

Isabella laughed. "Everyone knows Thomas. We like to eat breakfast on the patio where he plays his guitar." She hummed a few lines of a song I didn't recognize. "I always ask him to play my favorite song and he always does." Isabella slipped into the car with her mom and I knocked on the window.

Isabella," I said quickly. "Do you want to help with the sea star project Devon and I are working on? We are having a big

BioBlitz and we could use more help." I hadn't ever pictured myself being friends with Isabella. But I'd discovered that people had different parts to them. There was a story to everyone, and once they shared that story it was easier to understand them.

Isabella's eyes sparkled. "Sure! We'll be here for the summer and my dad works for a tech company in Seattle. I'll ask him to help us design an app just for the BioBlitz."

"Perfect!" I raised my hand in a high five and Isabella's palm smacked mine in a resounding yes.

"I'll text you about the common murre," Isabella said. "See you later!" She waved her hand out the window and this time, unlike all the Saturdays at SEALS, I waved back and yelled, "See you later!"

15

INSPECTION

The heavy rain swept over the yard and sounded like soldiers marching on our roof. A small trickle of water poured out of the gutters and splashed into a standing puddle by cottage four. It had been raining for three days straight in heavy sheets that blew across the town and made me not want to go outside. We only had one set of guests and Mom had moved them from cottage four yesterday after they checked in and complained the roof was leaking onto their floor. Luckily it was a Tuesday, and even though it was mid-June, the cottages were not all full. Maybe people knew that summer didn't really start until July Fourth on the Oregon Coast and there was still the possibility of drenchers in June.

Mom called Uncle Isaac to see about fixing the leak. I thought he might not want to come over in the middle of a huge downpour, but he did, and after he took a look at the leak and decided he needed a few more things to fix it, the two of them had found the plastic Adirondack chairs we usually kept around the firepit and had moved them to sit under the eaves of our house. Mom had a soft, dreamy look on her face and Uncle Isaac sat very close to Mom and touched her hand as he talked.

"Lucy," Mom called through the open kitchen window where I stood over the sink. "Uncle Isaac and I are going to run to the superstore and pick up a few things."

"Sure." I dumped a stack of mussels into a pan of hot soapy water. Mom and Uncle Isaac did a lot of errands together. They also usually took longer than they said because Uncle Isaac liked to take detours and sit at the beach and watch the waves with Mom. Mom thought it was very romantic. I wished they would just do the errands and come home.

I ran my hands under the hot water and soaped the mussels. I had been collecting them on my walks with Luna. Almost all the rocks were covered in mussels, and although we weren't allowed to collect mussels, or anything, from Sea Rock, people still picked them off the other rocks on the north and south ends and left them lying on the sand.

Mom and Uncle Isaac got into his truck and pulled out of our gravel parking lot. As I washed the mussels, I thought about what we still needed to do for the sea star research. Devon and I had pretty much concluded that the wasting syndrome had taken out eighty percent of the population at Sea Rock, but I still needed to do one more sea star survey to gather data before the BioBlitz.

Isabella and I had worked together to learn the new app which would be used in the BioBlitz. Her dad had been happy to help us, and after a couple glitches, we got everything working. The BioBlitz would take place after July Fourth. It was only a small segment of the Oregon Coast, but hopefully it would be enough to start making people aware of the plight of the sea stars. We wanted to let people to know about the sea star wasting syndrome up and down the coast with more

BioBlitzes and citizen science projects. Everyone needed to be involved to help save the sea stars.

Luna stirred and whined. She walked to the door and pawed the wood paneling. "What's up girl?" I peered out the kitchen window. A man in a long black trench coat walked up our pathway. Luna whined louder.

Forgetting about turning off the kitchen faucet, I opened the side door. Luna bounded out.

"Thomas! Thomas!" I cried.

Thomas knelt to hug Luna. His body wrapped around hers. For a minute, sadness washed over me. Luna was Thomas's dog and I was only fostering her. But in the past two weeks, I'd gotten so used to having Luna around me I forgot she didn't really belong to me.

"Come in!" I held open the door. "It's pouring."

Luna trotted inside and turned as if to say to Thomas, "You are coming, aren't you?"

Rain dripped off Thomas's coat as he stepped into the kitchen. He shivered. "Thanks for taking care of Luna for me."

"You're shivering. You should take a hot shower." Hot showers always warmed me up after I had been at SEALS in the cold and rain. I checked the clock. It was at least a thirty-minute drive to the superstore and back, plus the shopping time, and then if Uncle Isaac and Mom stopped to see the ocean waves, it would be another thirty minutes or so. Thomas had plenty of time to take a shower before Mom got home.

I eyed the bathroom Mom and I shared. I didn't think it was a good idea to let him take a shower in our bathroom. Mom was picky about that kind of thing and I knew she'd find a stray hair or something and know I had let him shower there.

I grabbed the clipboard by the door which listed the

cottages and dates of guests with small check marks by arrival or departure. "Cottage four doesn't have any guests. There was a small leak last night, so no one will be checking in anytime soon," I said. "You could use that shower. It's one of the dog-friendly units," I continued, as if I was checking in a guest. "And Luna will have a dog bed to rest on. I'll get one of the pet baskets, so she has some treats too."

"Thanks so much, Lucy," Thomas said. "I do feel a little chilled."

"Of course," I told Thomas, glad that I could be helpful like everyone else at Sea Rock Cove. I grabbed the number four key from the key ring behind the front door and a blue pet basket from the shelf above the door. Mom had placed a couple of old towels in each to dry sandy paws, a small bag of dog treats and a laminated sheet about the pet rules of the cottages. I also picked up a couple of fresh towels from the laundry room for Thomas.

I led Thomas and Luna down the courtyard pathway and up to the cottage door. The key slid easily inside. When we got inside, Luna sniffed everything and then turned around and lay down on the dog bed.

"I'll come check on you in a little while," I said, sounding like Mom as I exited the cottage and shut the door behind me. Thomas should have plenty of time to take a hot shower. Afterwards, he could sit outside with Luna in the chairs under the eaves. We had kept Luna for two weeks and this was her sometimes home now.

When I got back inside our house, the kitchen sink was overflowing and the water ran down the sides of the counter-top. Pools of water lay on the kitchen floor. I yelped and turned off the faucet. I had left it running when Thomas arrived and although it wasn't on full force, it had been enough of a stream to make everything overflow to the floor.

The doorbell rang as I finished mopping the floor with thick towels from the laundry room. Most of the guests didn't ring our doorbell. They texted or called Mom if they needed something.

I danced to the front door and opened it. The rain had stopped, at least for now. A tall man wearing khaki pants, loafers and a button-down white dress shirt stood in front of me with a clipboard. "Can I help you?" I asked.

"I'm the county inspector, Rick Santanio. I'm here to inspect the cottages for their annual review." Mr. Santanio had dark brown hair with streaks of grey along the temples and a receding hairline. He looked like he had a nice office job in one of the buildings at Seaman Point where all the county offices were located. The city code manager had visited the cottages a couple of times to make sure Mom had adequate parking, or to check on the signage for the tsunamis and see if it was placed in all the cottages on the back of the doors. The city code manager always wore jeans, a flannel shirt and a cap on his head. He was much less official and more like a friendly neighbor stopping by to see if you needed help with anything.

"Did my mom expect you, Mr. Santanio?" I placed my hands on my hips and stood in the doorway. I tried to sound like an adult, and sometimes I heard Mom use people's last names when she wanted to show she couldn't be bossed around. "We have guests." I pictured Thomas taking his shower, and cottage one, the family with the dog and the leaking roof. The inspector couldn't just barge in on them.

"I notified the owners." Mr. Santanio consulted his clipboard. "It looks like the owners live in Arizona?"

"Yes," I said. "Mom and I manage the cottages." I smiled at him. "We're making sure the bunnies are not being fed. It's a new ordinance in the town."

"That's nice," Mr. Santanio said. "Do you have a set of keys I could use?"

"The cottages have guests," I repeated. "I don't think the guests would like someone barging into their space when they are on vacation." I lowered my voice. "They could be doing anything."

Mr. Santanio studied me for a minute. It was the look teachers sometimes gave me when I pushed too far. "I will make sure the guests are aware of my presence." He waved at the blue sky. "Rain stopped. I'm sure your guests, if they are in the cottages, wouldn't mind going to the beach while I take a look around."

Mom was not going to like this, but I didn't have any choice. I didn't want Mr. Santanio to call the police and have them arrest me for obstruction of the inspection. I'd heard about these things on the late-night TV shows Mom liked to watch. It ended up being part of a master scheme for some crime that had been committed. I grabbed the keys from Mom's desk drawer and handed them to him. "Are you inspecting this house too?" I asked. I hoped not. Mom had been so busy with guests, we didn't have time to clean our own house. Laundry was piled in a big basket by the washing machine, dust bunnies floated under the couch and tables, and sand particles nestled between the crevices of the wood floors.

"Just the cottages," Mr. Santanio said. "It won't take me long."

He turned and headed toward cottage six. When he reached cottage six, he knocked sharply on the door and waited. No one was there, so it didn't take him long to open the door and step inside. I went back to my clean-up work in the kitchen. Thomas and Luna would be fine. The inspector would knock, and they would answer the door like any other guests.

By the time I finished cleaning the kitchen, Mom appeared at the door. "Lucy, can you help me unload the car?"

"That was fast." I tossed the rag into the laundry room.

"We didn't go all the way to the superstore in Seaman Point. We just ran up to the grocery store in Pelican Shores. They had pretty much everything we needed."

I followed Mom to Uncle Isaac's truck at the back of the house, in a small alleyway where we kept the trash and where she unloaded her groceries. "Where's Uncle Isaac?" I hefted a sack of paper towels and toilet paper into my arms.

"He went to check on the leak in cottage four." Mom's face got that dreamy look again. "He's so nice to spend all this time helping us."

"Cottage four?" I dropped the bag on the counter and raced for the door.

But I knew I was too late. The front door of cottage four stood open, Uncle Isaac and Mr. Santanio talked in loud voices. I pushed past them. My stomach balled into a rock of tension.

In the bedroom, Thomas lay sprawled across the bed snoring loudly. Luna sat in the dog bed, her eyes open, staring at the two men in the doorway. She didn't move from Thomas's bedside, not even for me.

"Lucy," Mom grabbed my shoulder from behind in a tight grip. "What is going on?"

"It was raining." I squirmed under the pressure. "Thomas was cold. I let him take a shower. He wasn't supposed to take a nap. But I guess he was tired. He's been sick …" My heart pounded. I wanted to help Thomas. But Mom was in big trouble. I could see it on Mr. Santanio's face. And if Mom was in trouble, it meant we were in trouble.

"Are you Mrs. Lavender, the manager?" Mr. Santanio asked Mom.

Mom's face turned white. "Yes." She pushed her lips so far into her mouth I thought they might be gone.

"I'm afraid I have to shut you down. This cottage has a leaking roof and you have a homeless man who seems to be living here. All of which is unsanitary and dangerous for visiting guests. Until these things can be fixed and changed, we will declare this as closed for business."

"How do you know Thomas is houseless?" I placed my hands on my hips. "Maybe he is a paying guest."

"I told him." Uncle Isaac dropped his head and stared at the ground. "I was so surprised to see Thomas and then I explained who he was."

"But Thomas is not living there." I pushed past Mom. "He just took a shower. He was cold and wet."

"Lucy!" Mom's voice arched in a sharp command.

I closed my mouth and swallowed the rest of my words. I knew not to make it worse and it was already bad. Very bad. The owner was not going to be happy with Mom as manager, and she would lose her job and we'd have to move. Sea Rock Cove and Pelican Shores didn't have a lot of jobs open at this time of the year that paid enough for Mom and me to live on. By now, all the hotel manager jobs were filled for the season. And even if she got a job as a hotel room cleaner, there weren't a lot places we could afford to rent in Sea Rock Cove. People made more money renting their cottages to the visitors for the summer and fall then they could renting them to the locals who needed rental housing. My stomach churned in that way it did when the police officer came to tell Mom that Dad had died.

"Is there something we can do? It's almost the Fourth of July. The cottages are booked for weeks. It's seasonal and this is high season." Uncle Isaac clenched his left fist and dropped his right arm across Mom's shoulder in a protective embrace.

"I'm afraid not." Mr. Santanio whipped out his phone and noted a few things. He reached into his satchel, walked to the vine-covered entryway and hung a closed sign. "I will need you to cancel your reservations. I will notify the owner. You are out of compliance with the county codes and until this all gets straightened out and the fines paid, you will be closed to guests."

Luna walked to me and nuzzled Mom's hand, as if she knew she needed comfort more than Thomas right now.

Thomas stood in the doorway to the bedroom, his eyes etched with sadness. "I'm sorry."

I clenched my fists. I was sorry Thomas had to apologize. Sea Rock Cove had all these homes that were for people to rent who visited for a week, and they belonged to people who already had other homes. But Thomas didn't even have one home. And now Mom and I didn't have a home either.

* * *

AFTER THE INSPECTOR LEFT, Mom and Uncle Isaac sat on the couch and talked in very low whispers as they studied the computer with all the reservations. Thomas and Luna had left right after the inspector gave Mom the yellow slip of paper from his tablet with all the code violations, fines, and where to appear in the county court to pay them. I picked up my back-pack and headed to the beach. I had to do the sea star survey, even if the tide wasn't low enough. I would have to wade into the water and try to do the count. We had to get the numbers before Mom and I left Sea Rock Cove.

A light rain blew across the beach and the thick grey clouds hovered above me. The tide was coming in and swirled around Sea Rock. I knew it wasn't the right time to do the survey. I would have to wade into the foaming water and then stand there while the water swirled around me to count the sea stars. I had my wader boots that Glory had given me, but the tide was high and the cold water would easily come up to the tops or over and into my boots.

The beach was empty with the exception of one person walking a dog up towards the north end. I gritted my teeth and stepped into the swirling water. It came up to the edges of my waders, but I kept pressing forward until I reached the right side of Sea Rock. The rip tides were strongest here and last summer a girl had drowned, but I tried not to think about it. I was a good swimmer. I opened my backpack, holding it above the water and pulled out my small flashlight and clipboard with the sea star survey paper attached.

A surging wave crashed against the back of my legs, and I gripped the edges of Sea Rock to steady myself. My hands held onto the mussels and a few broke off into the water.

Once the wave subsided in the receding tide, I held the flashlight close to Sea Rock and counted the baby sea stars. Another wave lapped at the edges of my boots and the water poured over the tops and inside. I shivered in the cold as the rain came down harder across my face.

Count. I told myself. Just count the sea stars.

I had almost reached the end of my counting. I just needed to kneel to get a little closer when a large wave slammed into my back. I stumbled and couldn't keep my footing. The flashlight flew out of my hands and the clipboard landed in the water with a thump. The water rushed around me as I went down in the wave, bouncing against Sea Rock and swallowing cold salt water. I knew the water wasn't that deep. Only up to my knees. But now the waves rushed around me and my clothes weighed me down. I tried to shrug out of my backpack but I couldn't move my arms. Another big wave cascaded over me, this one crashing over my head, and I went under the water.

I swallowed more salt water and struggled to the surface, coughing and coughing. My forehead slammed against Sea Rock.

Suddenly, hands grabbed me and pulled me out of the water.

"Lucy!"

I heard my name, but it sounded very far away and I couldn't answer. I felt dizzy and closed my eyes to stop the sky from swirling around me as the man and his dog pulled me along the sand and toward Sea Rock Cove. In a haze, I felt the world drift away from me.

When I opened my eyes again, I lay on a couch with a thick, dark red blanket over me. More blankets were tucked around my legs and side. I was encased in the warm cocoon. Max sat beside me in a rocking chair with a cup of tea at his side. Honeybear lay beside me on the floor by the couch.

"There you are," he said, and leaned down to touch my forehead. "Looks like you bumped your head on Sea Rock. It's going to be a nasty bruise."

I struggled to sit up. "What time is it?"

"Noon," Max said.

"It's only been thirty minutes since I went out to Sea Rock?" I rubbed my head where a big headache was starting.

"It can seem like forever when you get caught in one of those rip tides," Max said. "But you were lucky Honeybear and I were walking by. You're going to be okay. Just a nasty bruise on your forehead."

I sat up and the morning disaster rushed back to me. "No, I'm not." I pulled the heavy red blanket closer to me. "Everything is not okay." In a rush I told Max what had happened that morning. I told him about Thomas and how I'd let him take a shower, and how Mom had gone to the store with Uncle Isaac and the inspector had come by and shut us down. I told him how the BioBlitz was coming, and that I had to be here to do it with Devon and Isabella, and how Devon and I were going to go to Heron Junior High together and we were best friends, and how I'd never had a best friend because we moved so much. By the time I finished, the tears were pouring down my cheeks.

Max leaned down close to me. "Sea Rock Cove is your home, Lucy Lavender. We'll make sure you and your Mom have a place to live in Sea Rock Cove."

"Everything is hopeless," I sobbed. "There isn't anything anyone can do." I turned my face away from Max to the painting over the fireplace. A purple sea star with exactly the same white pattern on its back as the sea star Dad had tattooed on his arm stared back at me. Dad always said the pattern was unique to him. The white dots formed his initials.

I turned to Max. "You are my grandpa." I said softly.

Max looked for a minute at the painting and then turned back to me. "Yes," he said. "I am."

I reached into my t-shirt to hold onto my sea star necklace, but it was gone.

16
TRUTH

I pulled the covers up around me, shivering. It wasn't that I was cold. It felt very warm and cozy in Max's living room, with the stacks of art books on coffee tables and a half-finished painting on an easel. The room was painted a light yellow and a red Oriental rug covered the hardwood floor. A stone fireplace that stretched floor to ceiling took up the left wall. A handful of what looked like old photos decorated the mantel. Was Dad in any of those pictures?

"If you're my grandpa …" I fiddled with the blanket's edges. "Why did Dad say you died?"

Max leaned back in his rocking chair and stared at the painting of the sea star. "Your dad and I had a big falling out when he turned eighteen. I wanted him to work in the hotel industry. I owned three resort hotels along the coast and I hoped to make him partner one day."

"But Dad wanted to work in marine biology," I said. "He went to Alaska and worked on the fishing boat until he met Mom, because it was how he could be close to the sea." I felt as if the world tilted underneath me. Which story was true about Dad?

"Yes," Max said. "Your dad loved the sea. But he had some problems with high school. He didn't make the best grades. When it came time to apply for college, he didn't have the grades to go and do what he wanted to do."

I pushed the blanket off me and swung my legs over the couch, hoping to steady myself. Dad always seemed smart to me. He was the one who had taught me about the sea. He bought me the marine biology coloring book and worked with me on it at night. He loved to put together puzzles that were pictures of sea turtles moving through the ocean waters.

Max faced me and leaned forward. "I thought if your dad worked at the hotel, got to know all the roles, took some classes at the community college in hospitality, he could still be close to the ocean and that would be enough for him." His voice filled with a deep sadness. "But it was my dream, not his."

"And he left?" I asked.

"He took a job in Alaska on a fishing boat," Max said. "I took it as a personal failing that my son didn't want to go into the industry where I had built my life." Max shook his head. "Your Aunt Charlotte warned me that life didn't last forever. She told me I should let go of my pride and get a hold of your Dad. But I couldn't. I always thought there would be more time. Time to make up with each other ..." Max's voice trailed off.

I leaned back against the thick couch pillows. "Did you know about me?"

Max nodded. "Your Aunt Charlotte always told me what you were doing. I asked her to call your mom every Sunday and tell me everything."

My face flushed as I remembered those voice messages

that Mom never responded to. All those calls she didn't return, where Max didn't get to hear about me. "Does Mom know you're my grandfather?"

Max shook his head. "Your dad wanted her to believe I was dead. I have never met her."

"Did you find Mom the job at the cottages or was it Aunt Charlotte?" I asked.

"Me," Max said. "I know most of the hotel owners up and down the coast. When I heard that the cottages needed a new manager, I told the owner I knew of someone. I wanted your mom and you close. I hoped one day I could get to know you."

My heart closed up with tears. Max did want to know his granddaughter. Me.

Max put his head in his hands and his shoulders shook. "I'm sorry, Lucy. I can't make up to you what has happened with your dad and not getting to know you, but I hope from here forward we can change that."

An image flashed across my mind. I saw myself standing at Sea Rock that first day and talking to Max about how we liked to study Sea Rock. "We both like Sea Rock," I said, and smiled.

"We do," Max said.

"But it doesn't matter," I said. "Mom and I don't have a place to live in Sea Rock Cove anymore. Mom doesn't have a job."

"I know. I can't change the codes or rules, and unfortunately, I can't insist that the owner of the cottages keep your Mom on as manager. That's his business. But that doesn't mean you have to leave Sea Rock Cove."

"Yes it does," I said. "We can't live here." I waved my hand around the small apartment that was tucked behind the art gallery. "There isn't a job for Mom that will pay enough to keep us living here. There aren't many places for rent and it's really expensive."

Max stared at the ground and toed a scratched spot on the hardwood floor.

I pushed back the heavy blankets. "I need to go home," I said. "Mom will be worried." I stood up and walked over to Max. I placed my hand on his shoulder. "Thank you for rescuing me."

Max looked up at me. "Of course," he said. "I dried your backpack and papers on the front table by the heater. They should be ready to go now."

I stared at the painting above the fireplace and the colorful sea stars around the base of Sea Rock. My neck felt empty and lost without my necklace. "I lost my sea star necklace," I said. "It must have fallen off in the water."

Max stood and walked to a sideboard. He pulled out the top drawer and removed a small box. "It looked like this."

I walked over and stared into the box. A necklace just like mine lay in white cotton.

"We used to sell them at the hotels," Max said, holding it out to me. "When you showed it to me on the beach that day, I recognized it. Your dad must have had one that he gave to you. He loved the sea stars. I spent hours with your dad at Sea Rock when he was a child. We learned the colors of the sea stars and how to count them."

Slowly I took the box. I didn't put the necklace on and held the box in my hand. My sea star necklace wasn't just connected to Dad. It was connected to Max, my grandpa.

"Thank you." I walked over to the front table where Max had set up a small space heater underneath. The sea star survey was crinkly but it was readable. I folded it and tucked it into the outside pocket of my backpack along with the sea star necklace box. I stepped into my waders which had also dried. Max handed me my coat and opened the door. Honeybear stood by his side.

"Max?" I asked. "Can I still call you Max? I don't think I'm ready to call you Grandpa." The word felt funny on my tongue.

"Of course," Max said, and smiled. "Max is fine for as long as you want to call me Max."

"See you later, Max." I waved and stepped out the door and headed toward the cottages. My step felt just a little stronger than it had a few hours ago when everything seemed to be crashing in. I couldn't wait to get home and chat with Devon and tell him that I had met my grandfather.

* * *

ON THE MORNING of the town's annual Fourth of July parade, the last thing I felt like doing was celebrating. But Devon and I had been talking about walking in the festival's parade for weeks. We wanted to hand out information about the upcoming BioBlitz. The app was finished and we were ready to roll out the BioBlitz, even if I wasn't sure if I could be a part of it now. Max had been able to convince the owner of the cottages to allow Mom and me to stay until after the holiday. In the last couple of weeks, Max had brought dinner over to Mom and me almost every night. At first, he just left meals at the door to our house, but after two nights, Mom said he should eat with us. We were family. Max didn't talk much during those dinners, but I liked having him at the table. It almost felt like Dad was there with us again.

The night before the parade, Isabella had Devon, Sofia, Martina and me over to make candy in sea star molds to hand out at the parade. We got to cook in Isabella's big kitchen and even though some of the candy overflowed from the pan onto the stove, Isabella's mom hadn't minded. After the candy hardened, we stuck it into small bags and attached index cards about the BioBlitz to them with thin ribbons.

Sea Rock Cove's parade encouraged everyone who wanted to participate to sign up, and lots of different groups of people took part. Aunt Charlotte said the best was always the Dove Street Chair Brigade. An entire street of people opened and closed folding chairs in a little rhythm while they walked. I hoped Devon and I were behind them.

The parade sign-up sheet was almost full when I added our names. When I finished, I headed into the open garage behind City Hall. The city vehicles were parked in the parking lot and Autumn had spread out material for a beach trash mural project onto several tables. She had an empty window frame on one table and buckets of microplastics on the others. Inside the window frame was a drawing of Sea Rock on a piece of plywood. People could stick the microplastics into the drawing and when it was finished, Autumn would seal everything with resin and auction it off for funding for SEALS education projects.

Outside of the garage, the SEALS truck was decorated with red, white and blue streamers and balloons. Kyra's car pulled into the parking lot as I grabbed another handful of microplastics. By the time I had the small pieces sorted by colors, Dylan rolled to my side. Red, white and blue ribbons were woven into the spokes of his chair's wheels and he wore a tall red and white hat with a blue shirt. His eyes sparkled.

"I signed us up for the parade." I stuck a small orange microplastic piece into the shape of a sea star leg on the mural.

"I've got the candy." Devon patted the tan sack attached to the back of his wheelchair.

. . .

THE MAYOR STOOD in the middle of the street outside City Hall. He blew a whistle and people sorted themselves into a line. I followed the numbers pasted on the street with blue tape. Devon and I were in the middle of the parade with the walking groups, and the cars were all in the front. The chair brigade was right behind us!

"Don't forget your beach shift," Autumn called to me from the open back end of the SEALS truck as they drove slowly past to line up with the cars.

"I won't!"

Sea Rock Cove didn't have fireworks. The eggs on Sea Rock had just hatched and if the parents left the burrows because they were frightened by the fireworks, predators like the eagles would get the pufflings and other young birds. During the afternoon shift, it would be my job to tell people they had to go to one of the neighboring towns if they wanted to see fireworks. Glory said most people didn't mind, but some got upset because they hadn't realized Sea Rock Cove didn't have fireworks. Max was going to volunteer, too, and I told Glory I would just get Max to tell them. He was good at looking scary.

It took a while for the parade to start moving, but pretty soon we were walking down the street. Devon rolled up to people on the sidewalks and tossed handfuls of the sea star candy into the air. I called out, "Help us save the sea stars! Come to the BioBlitz!"

We moved into the downtown area, where every business had hung a banner flag and small American flags lined the sidewalks. As we approached, people cheered, I knew they were cheering for the chair brigade behind us, but it felt nice to think they might be cheering for us one day, after we saved the sea stars.

A bearded, heavyset man reached out his hand for a piece

of candy and I scooped one out of Devon's bag and handed it to him. He looked at the attached index card and tore it off. Then he crumpled it and stepped on it. "You can't save the sea stars," he said. His dark eyes flashed at me.

"Yes, we can," I said. "We can all save them."

Devon rolled over to me. "What's going on?"

The man looked at Devon and shook his head. "Bet *you* think you can save the sea stars too?"

"We *are* saving the sea stars." Devon's voice held strong and firm. "One step at a time."

"I've been surfing in these waters for years. The problem is way too big for all of us. We're just doomed." The man chewed on the candy.

"I'm sorry you think that way." I repeated the line they taught me to say at SEALS to guests who disagreed.

Devon twirled his chair and tossed another piece of candy toward the man. "Enjoy."

Devon and I moved with the parade past the Bow Wow pet store. "Some people are just always going to see the negative. No matter what you say or do. I'm glad you're my friend, Lucy. You always find the good."

"So do you," I said. And it was true. I never heard Devon complain. He was sad sometimes, but sad and complaining were two different things.

Ahead of us, Thomas and Luna walked across the middle of the street, cutting through the parade to get to the restaurant. He carried his guitar on his back and Luna wore a red, white and blue bandanna around her neck. Thomas wore a red t-shirt, and his big, red and white and blue hat. He turned and saw me and waved a big, long wave.

I hadn't seen Thomas since he fell asleep in the cottage and I was glad to see him at the parade. I couldn't wait to tell him about Max. But, I smiled, thinking back to the first day I talked to Thomas, he already knew Max was my grandpa.

The parade looped off Main Street and headed back toward City Hall. By the time we got back, the chair brigade behind us didn't sound so good anymore. A few of them had dropped off when we passed their street and some of the others were only walking with their chairs held in front of them.

Devon and I met up with Kyra, Autumn, Angelina and Martina in front of the SEALS truck.

Glory stood in the back of the truck bed. "Listen up, everyone!" She waved her hands in the air. "This is it. It's time for me to announce some big news."

"We're all ears!" Autumn called. "But hurry up. I have to get back to the mural before people start trying to make their own pictures!"

Glory swallowed hard. "Oh gosh." She ducked her head. "I didn't know this was going to be hard. I didn't know ..."

"Tell us!" Kyra yelled.

"Okay." Glory wiped her eyes with the back of her hand. "I'm going to Australia."

"Whoooh!" Angelina tossed her hands in the air and gave a big shout-out.

"I'm not coming back." Glory looked at me. "I bought a one-way ticket. Something tells me I gotta go. There's something there for me I need to see or do. I don't know what. But you just have to follow that hunch when it comes up."

A lump formed in my throat. I knew Glory's dream was to go to Australia for her surfing magazine. I was happy for her. But I hadn't realized she wasn't going to come back. She wouldn't be there on the beach anymore with me. There would be someone else, someone without her pink fluffy earmuffs that she wore no matter what the weather.

Someone tapped my shoulder. I whirled around.

"Lucy," Aunt Charlotte said. "It's time to go." She wore a festive red, white and blue fancy scarf tied around her neck and a white scoop blouse with khaki pants. She even had sparkly red, white and blue sandals. But for all that sparkle and bling, she looked more like a stern teacher when the class was in trouble, and not someone who was celebrating the Fourth of July at the beach.

"But I'm volunteering for the shift at Sea Rock," I said. "I can't leave now."

"Yes." Aunt Charlotte placed her hand on my shoulder. "It's time to go."

I knew not to argue. Even though Max spent more and more time with us, Aunt Charlotte and Mom still kept their distance. I was pretty sure Aunt Charlotte would never understand Mom and me. I got my bike and Aunt Charlotte walked over to Kyra and said a few things. Kyra looked at me and nodded. She smiled a sad smile.

I walked my bike up the hill and toward the cottages. All around us, people packed up chairs and blankets and candy from the parade. They laughed and chatted about how this had been the best parade yet. A couple of people reached out to talk to Aunt Charlotte as we passed them. She smiled and nodded and said we needed to get going.

When we got to the cottages, I leaned my bike against our house and opened the back door. Mom sat at the kitchen table. She held a cup of coffee in her hands. Her face was calm, but her hands shook. "Lucy," she said, "we will need to leave tomorrow morning. They have hired a new manager and want a day to clean the house before he arrives."

My stomach clenched. "But you don't have a job anywhere else. Where are we going?" The last time, we had lived in our car for three months before Mom found another job and we saved up enough money for a deposit on an apartment.

"Aunt Charlotte has offered to let us live with her for a few days," Mom said. "And then we'll see. It's always good to move to new places."

I knew that wasn't the truth at all. Mom liked Sea Rock Cove. She and Uncle Isaac had a close friendship and she wanted to stay as much as I did. Devon and I were best friends and we were going to do the BioBlitz. And Max was in Sea Rock Cove. I had lost Dad but I had found Max, my grandfather.

Sea Rock Cove was home for both of us.

17

COURAGE

I carried my science box into the second-story blue and white bedroom at Aunt Charlotte's. A picture window overlooked a spacious garden. The garden bloomed with pink and blue hydrangeas. A thick blue bedspread lay over a queen-size bed filled with pillows of all shapes and sizes. A painting of the ocean hung on the wall behind the bed. I opened an armoire and placed my science box inside. I didn't bother to unpack my sack of clothing. We weren't going to stay long enough.

I wandered out of the room and down the long hallway. There were two more bedrooms. One, Aunt Charlotte used for her office, with a mahogany desk that had two computers. The second bedroom, Mom was going to sleep in. She had opened the sunny yellow blinds. The room had a big antique dresser with a white pitcher filled with hydrangeas. More art hung on the walls, but these watercolors showed sunny meadows and fields filled with flowers. Mom's duffle bag sat on the floor. She hadn't unpacked anything either.

The plush carpet barely moved under my feet as I made my

way downstairs and past the baby grand piano in the spacious living room. The room's double doors opened onto a sweeping back deck that overlooked the ocean. Mom sat in one of the chairs. She had a blanket tossed over her legs and stared into the ocean's crashing waves.

The smell of barbecued chicken drifted from the kitchen and I wandered into the large room. It was a lot like Isabella's kitchen when we cooked the sea star candy, with tons of white cabinets, silver appliances and two stoves. Aunt Charlotte had set a basket of rolls and some watermelon on a long counter. I licked my lips. I hadn't eaten anything since breakfast and my stomach grumbled. Aunt Charlotte's back was turned to me as she cut slices of cheese and placed it on a plate.

I snuck a piece of watermelon out of a bowl and slipped it into my mouth.

Aunt Charlotte turned. "Lucy," she said. "You scared me." She placed her hand to her chest. "Are you hungry?"

"Kinda," I shrugged. I should have been very hungry, but something else rattled around in my stomach. Something that wasn't hunger at all, but more like fear and anger and worry all wrapped in one big bundle of a knot.

Aunt Charlotte had never been homeless or without a job. She sold expensive second homes to people who came out to the beach a handful of times or rented the homes out to visitors. She traveled a lot in the winter and went to her friends' homes in Hawaii and Arizona and California. Her holiday cards showed pictures of her on warm beaches.

Something inside me rumbled. I didn't want food.

I wanted Aunt Charlotte to open her eyes and look around and see the town where she lived. I wanted her to see beyond the fancy houses and the beach cottages that people only sometimes lived in. I wanted her to see people like Martina and Angelina. I wanted her to know that people like Mom and me used the food closet because we didn't have enough money to make it to the end of the month, even though Mom had a job. I wanted her to see that Thomas wasn't a dirty homeless person. He was someone who got hooked on drugs because he had physical pain. I wanted her to see we were all people doing our very best, and we all lived in Sea Rock Cove, just like her.

And then I remembered Isabella and how, once I knew her story, I understood her better. Aunt Charlotte didn't know how Mom and I lived. Mom had avoided Aunt Charlotte. She said we could handle it. But right now, we couldn't handle it. We were about to be houseless again until Mom could find another job. And who knew when that might be.

"Aunt Charlotte?" I took a deep breath and tried to calm my fast-beating heart.

Aunt Charlotte turned to me.

"I don't want food." I swallowed. "I have something to tell you."

"Is your room okay?" Aunt Charlotte asked.

"That's not it." I took a deep breath of courage. "Sometimes Mom and I don't have a place to live."

Aunt Charlotte set her plate of cheese down with a loud *thunk* on the granite counter. "What are you telling me, Lucy Lavender?"

The story poured out of me. How hard it had been in the last three years since Dad died. Mom was trying to take online classes and get her business associate degree. But her jobs didn't pay enough for us to pay rent and have enough left over for everything else. I told Aunt Charlotte about Mom's housecleaning job, and how she got sick and couldn't work for a week and we had to leave in the middle of the night because Mom couldn't pay the rent; how she hadn't been able to find another job right away and we lived in our car with a group of other people in a camp near the Portland airport.

Aunt Charlotte sat down on one of the stools at the kitchen counter. She placed her face in her hands. Sometimes tears pooled in her eyes. But I kept talking until the whole story was out.

"I'm so sorry," Aunt Charlotte said. Her voice cracked. "I called every Sunday and tried to talk to your Mom, but I guess I really didn't understand what was going on in your lives. We think people are fine because I guess it's easier that way. We don't get close enough to find out otherwise."

"Mom and I don't want to leave Sea Rock Cove." I placed my hands on the counter to steady myself. Mom wasn't going to like it that I had told Aunt Charlotte everything, but we needed her help. We couldn't keep moving around and living out of our car when Mom didn't have work. Max had tried to find us a place to live but there wasn't anyone in town who had an available, affordable space for us. No one except...I eyed the expansive home. Aunt Charlotte. Aunt Charlotte was family and in hard times family supported each other; that's what I'd learned at Sea Rock Cove. "Maybe we could live with you?" I held my breath as the words burst out of me.

Aunt Charlotte picked up the plate of crackers and cheese and threw back her shoulders. "I'm going to talk to your mom for a while."

I trailed after her into the living room and sank into the white couch with the thick pillows.

I stared at the full bookcases. Aunt Charlotte didn't have any science books. Everything was art and design, travel and popular literature. Occasionally, I peered out the windows to the porch. Both Mom and Aunt Charlotte had moved their chairs and had their backs to me. But Mom was eating the cheese and crackers.

After what seemed like forever, they both stood and walked inside.

"We're going to make a plan," Aunt Charlotte said. "You can live here for as long as you need. We can change things around. If Lucy wants room for her science experiments, we can make room. You are my niece, Lucy, and I want you and your mom to have a home, here in Sea Rock Cove. It's where you belong."

"You told her." Mom walked over to me and sank down on the couch beside me. She placed her hand on my leg.

"I had to, Mom." I said. "I don't want to leave Sea Rock Cove." I started to cry. "I have friends and I want to go to Heron Junior High and be in science club with Devon."

Mom hugged me hard. "We're not going to leave."

I wiped away the tears and took a tissue from Aunt Charlotte. "I can do my BioBlitz?"

"Yes." Aunt Charlotte snapped her fingers. "I'm going to announce the BioBlitz on the Chamber of Commerce website and email newsletter. I have some real estate clients who I'm sure would be happy to help you."

"Whoooh …" I jumped off the couch and looked at the grandfather clock. There was still time left in my shift at Sea Rock. "Can I go help at Sea Rock? They need me to help tell people about the no fireworks."

"Yes," Aunt Charlotte said. "Go on. And when you get home we'll have the best July Fourth picnic ever at the beach. I'll call Max and invite him too. It's time I spent a little more quality time with my dad, too." She handed me a big slice of watermelon and I grabbed another piece for Thomas.

I chomped the watermelon as I ran toward the restaurant where Thomas was playing his guitar. Aunt Charlotte lived just blocks away and I was there before I finished my slice.

"Thomas!" I said. "We're going to stay. It's all going to be okay. We're going to live with Aunt Charlotte for a while."

"That's great, Lucy Lavender." Thomas strummed a few beats of his guitar.

"Aunt Charlotte has friends who are going to help with the BioBlitz. I bet they could help you, too."

A shadow crossed Thomas's face. He stopped playing his guitar. "I really appreciate that, Lucy. But I don't need help. Luna and I are doing just fine."

"But Thomas," I said "Don't you want a home? Don't you want a warm place to sleep every night?" Why wouldn't Thomas want help? It didn't make any sense.

Thomas stared into the sky and then looked at me. "You know, Lucy Lavender? Sometimes things just need to remain the way they are. Sometimes people just have to go on doing what they're doing."

"But Thomas ..."

Thomas's gaze hardened.

I knew when to leave things alone and leaned over to pet Luna. Mom didn't want to tell Aunt Charlotte about our situation. Maybe it was the same with Thomas. It wasn't easy to admit you needed help. People wanted to figure things out on their own—and sometimes you just had to let them be. But it didn't mean you couldn't still care about them and keep offering that help.

"I'll be right back," I said and ran into the Bow Wow pet store. I grabbed one of the little pieces of paper that you filled out for your dog's name tag and sent it in and got back a gold circle to attach to their collar.

I jogged back outside to Thomas and Luna. "I'm getting Luna a tag," I said as I pressed firmly on the paper against the concrete wall beside the restaurant.

"Well," Thomas said. "That's awful nice of you."

"I'm going to put Aunt Charlotte's phone number on it," I said. "In case Luna gets lost, someone can call me."

Thomas blinked fast and said, his voice muffled, "Lucy Lavender, Sea Rock Cove is definitely your home."

"It sure is," I said as I finished filling out the paper and jumped up to give Luna a big hug. "It's all of our homes."

18

GOODBYE PUFFINS

*I*n the middle of August, Max helped Devon and me finish our study of the sea stars. We had documented the sea star numbers in a very well-attended BioBlitz, and people donated a lot of money to SEALS for more research. The SEALS program signed up new volunteers, and Aunt Charlotte started a special festival just to bring people's awareness to the problems in the ocean. Mom was working on her online business classes and had accepted a job working at the Chamber of Commerce. We were still going to live with Aunt Charlotte because we had found all of us liked living together. She had even added a few science books to her collection. Max came over for dinner a couple times a week, and every time he told stories about Dad. Stories about Dad as a child, just like me, growing up at Sea Rock Cove.

Even though Uncle Isaac wasn't doing the lawn work at the cottages anymore, he still visited Mom an awful lot—something that made her smile a lot more and laugh. I still didn't like his visits, but I liked how happy it made Mom.

In a few weeks, I would start seventh grade at Heron

Junior High. I was excited about being on the volleyball team with Martina and starting a new science club with Devon. Our new focus was going to be the birds of Sea Rock. The puffin numbers were declining, and we wanted to find out what we could do to save them. But the best part was that Devon would be attending Heron Junior High with me and we were in three classes together. We had already pledged to eat every lunch together.

Glory stood in the city parking lot by the SEALS truck. This afternoon was a solar eclipse we wanted to see together and her last shift. Tonight, she would drive to Portland and get on her one-way flight to Australia. She handed me her earmuffs.

"You should have these," she said. "There's a lot of cold shifts out on the beach and you need something to keep your ears warm." Tears poked at the corners of her eyes, but she brushed them away and smiled at me.

I took the earmuffs and, even though it was seventy degrees, placed them on my ears.

We got into the truck. Glory drove slowly on the beach and hung her fingers out the window. The season was winding down and they didn't need all the SEALS on the beach at every shift. "I'm really going to miss this," she said. "It's just one of those places that gets in your heart and stays there. No matter what."

I knew exactly what she meant.

At Sea Rock, Glory got out the box of eclipse viewing glasses. The news media had been warning everyone for weeks not to look at the sun when the solar eclipse happened. But I didn't think we were going to need them. A dense fog had moved across the beach. It was the fourth straight day of ninety-nine degrees in Portland, and the mountains had caused an inversion that trapped cooler air over Sea Rock Cove and we got socked in with fog.

The beach was mostly empty, as if people knew the solar eclipse couldn't be seen here today.

Glory looked at Sea Rock for a long time.

I let her have her space and took a pair of binoculars out of the truck. Common murres flew over my head in clusters.

I pointed the binoculars at the burrows of Sea Rock. Two puffins perched beside the grassy space and that was it.

"How many today?" Glory stepped up beside me.

"Two," I said. There wasn't anyone to see the puffins leave, not the way Glory and I had seen them arrive together with my entire class.

In the spring, the puffins would return to their same burrows to mate and the new season would start. It would be a different season without Glory. And Glory wasn't the only one who wouldn't return to SEALS. Isabella finally told her parents she didn't want to volunteer with the SEALS, but she promised Martina, Sofia and I that she would still see us around on weekends and summers when she visited Sea Rock Cove. And Max would be here. He walked the beach every day with Honeybear, rain or shine. Sometimes I walked with him, and on occasion, he even let me walk Honeybear.

And that's how it worked at Sea Rock Cove. The changes ebbed and flowed like the tides and no season was ever the same.

Glory dropped her arm around my shoulder. "Let's sing to the puffins."

Together, Glory and I raised our voices in song to the puffins as they flew out to sea.

AFTERWORD

Sea Star Wasting Syndrome (SSWS) is the largest marine disease outbreak ever documented in a non-commercial species. It occurred from 2013-2014 and stretched from Alaska to Baja, California. SSWS affected over twenty species. The ochre sea stars, found in the Oregon Coast intertidal zones, have not recovered, although there are some areas which are showing an improvement. The sunflower sea stars have become non-existent. Marine biologists are working to find answers, but the cause of sea star wasting syndrome and the outbreak are still unknown. For more information visit: www.seastarwasting.org.

How Can You Help?

The best way you can help the sea stars is to get involved with a coastal citizen science project to help document the sea stars and the sea star wasting syndrome through the Multi-Agency Rocky Intertidal Network. https://marine.ucsc.edu/data-products/sea-star-wasting/index.html

LUCY'S SEA ROCK GLOSSARY

Sea Rock Cove: Fictional town ninety miles west of Portland, Oregon, four hours south of Seattle, Washington.

Sea Rock: A fictional haystack rock in the Pacific Ocean, based on Haystack Rock in Cannon Beach, Oregon.

Seaman Point: Fictional town forty minutes north of Sea Rock Cove.

Pelican Shores: Fictional town fifteen minutes north of Sea Rock Cove.

Pelican Elementary School (K-6): Elementary school for students in both Sea Rock Cove and Pelican Shores, located in Pelican Shores.

Heron Junior High (7-8): Junior high school for students in Sea Rock Cove and Pelican Shores, located in Pelican Shores behind Pelican Elementary School.

Welcome Back Puffin Song: Students on the north Oregon Coast welcome back the tufted puffins each year with a field trip to Haystack Rock. "The Welcome Back Tufted Puffins" song is sung to the tune of "The Muffin Man."

What's Found at Sea Rock

Sea stack: Steep, vertical columns of rock near a coastline, formed by wave erosion.

Haystack Rock: A sea stack which looks like a large haystack, made of basalt rock and formed by molten lava. There are three haystack rocks on the Oregon Coast located in Cannon Beach, Pacific City and Bandon. On some maps, the Pacific City haystack rock is marked as Chief Kiawanda Rock. Haystack Rock in Cannon Beach is accessible by foot at low tides and was seen in the movie *The Goonies.*

SEALS: Sea Learning Specialists who work at Sea Rock.

Seabirds: Ocean dwelling birds that live off the sea, coming to land only to breed and raise their young. This includes most of the birds who dwell at Sea Rock, such as the tufted puffins and common murres.

Common murre: A seabird with white breast and black feathers. They cluster in tightly packed groups and lay one pear-shaped egg at a time, which is raised by the father. A common murre chick is called a "jumpling" because it jumps off cliffs to join its father in the water.

Pelagic cormorant: Seabirds with long sleek necks, glossy purple-black feathers, and white flank patches. They nest in loose colonies on narrow shelves of steep cliffs, in nests of seaweeds and grasses.

Black oystercatcher: Seabird with striking, bright red-orange bill and pink legs, commonly found along rocky intertidal shorelines. They nest in smooth depressions on rocky headlands. Breeding pairs aggressively defend their nests and their sharp piercing cry is distinct.

Tufted puffin: Stout, black-bodied seabird with large colorful bill of orange and yellow, and two yellow tufts on the head during breeding season. Fast wing fluttering which often looks like the common murre as they fly off to catch fish, but landings are awkward and clumsy. They dig burrows in grassy slopes, using the same burrow each season, and raise a single chick, called a "puffling," on small fish. Tufted puffins are often found in the northern Pacific Ocean rocky shore habitats and have a well-established burrow in Cannon Beach, Oregon at Haystack Rock.

Pigeon guillemot: Chunky birds in the same family as puffins. Smooth black plumage, white wing patches and bright red legs and feet make them easy to identify. Found on rocky cliffs. Both parents care for the young, who are fed sixteen times a day and triple their weight in ten days.

Western gull: Common white and grey seagull found in the ocean along the Oregon Coast.

Peregrine falcon: Natural predator of seabirds including the common murre and tufted puffin.

Bald eagle: Natural predator of seabirds including common murre and tufted puffin. Builds nest in trees near rocks where other birds nest.

What's Found in the Tide Pools?

Intertidal: Between the tides. The intertidal zone is the area of the seashore that is underwater at high tide and exposed during low tide. It can be divided into three smaller zones: high tide zone, mid tide zone and low tide zone. Each zone has different animals that are exposed to air for different lengths of time. Intertidal animals can survive out of water twice a day during low tide.

California mussels: Black shell-covered animals which attach themselves to rocks by secreting a liquid that hardens and forms a thread in sea water. They rely on this strong thread to stay attached to the rocks during heavy surf. Sea stars eat mussels, and without sea stars, the mussel population has increased. They are amazing cleaners of water; an individual can filter up to a half gallon of water every hour while feeding!

Gooseneck barnacles: Small shellfish that attach themselves to rocks or other hard surfaces in the intertidal zone. They eat during high tide by extending a sticky foot into the water to capture phytoplankton.

Pink coralline algae: Plants that grow on rocks in intertidal zones. Looks like pink moss between the barnacles.

Nudibranchs: Shell-less marine mollusks, often called sea slugs because they are similar in size to slugs found on land.

Shed their shells after larva stage.

Giant green anemone: Marine animal with a circle of tentacles around its mouth. Rarely moves from the place where it attaches itself early in life. Feeds on crabs, mussels, small fish and sea urchins, using the stinging cells found on its tentacles to paralyze its prey. When they are exposed at low tide, people often try to poke giant green anemones and force them to close.

Ochre sea star: Most common kind of sea star found along the intertidal zone of the north Oregon Coast, purple and orange in color. Sea stars have five or more arms radiating from their center. They do not have eyes or a brain but grab moving prey including crabs, snails, barnacles and mussels with their arms. They pump water in and out of their madreporite, or filter, to fill up their arms and feet allowing them to cling and move.

Sunflower sea star: Sea star species with up to 24 arms which has been wiped out along the Oregon Coast due to sea star wasting syndrome (SSWS). The species is considered critically endangered.

Sea Star Wasting Syndrome (SSWS): A disease of sea stars which causes lesions to form and tissue to decay around the lesions. Then the sea star's body begins to quickly break down and fall apart, and the animal dies. SSWS is the largest marine disease outbreak ever documented in a non-commercial species. It occurred from 2013-2014 and stretched from Alaska to Baja, California. SSWS affected over twenty species of sea stars.

ABOUT THE AUTHOR

Mindy Hardwick holds an MFA in Writing for Children and Young Adults from Vermont College. Her published books include: *Stained Glass Summer, Weaving Magic and Seymour's Secret.* She also writes sweet contemporary romance including her Cranberry Bay Series: *Sweetheart Cottage* and *Sweetheart Summer.* Mindy facilitated a poetry workshop for teens at Denney Juvenile Justice Center and wrote about the experience in her memoir, *Kids in Orange: Voices from Juvenile Detention.*

Mindy is an avid supporter of Haystack Rock in Cannon Beach, Oregon. She served on the Friends of Haystack Rock Board and you can still catch her on a nice day, volunteering for the Haystack Rock Awareness Program. Mindy has been an educator for over twenty-two years and currently teaches at an online high school in the Portland, Oregon area.

When she is not writing, teaching or volunteering, Mindy can often be found walking with her cocker spaniel, Stormy, on the north Oregon Coast beaches and dreaming up new story ideas. She loves to talk to schools and as a teacher herself knows her way around the tools of virtual learning as well as in person workshops. Visit her website: www.mindyhardwick.com to find out about new releases, upcoming events or to book her to speak to your class or school group.

Photo Credit: Haystack Rock Awareness Program

ALSO BY MINDY HARDWICK

Middle Grade

Stained Glass Summer

Seymour's Secret

Young Adult

Weaving Magic

Kids in Orange: Voices from Juvenile Detention

Sweet Contemporary Romance

Sweetheart Cottage

Sweetheart Summer

SEYMOUR'S SECRET

Enjoy an excerpt from Seymour's Secret

CHAPTER ONE: ROBBER

*O*ur front door was kicked in when we arrived home from Granddad's funeral.

"Colt!" Mom jerked her arm out in front of me like she does when the car makes a sudden stop. "Don't go in."

I kicked the snow off my boots, leaving thick dirty clumps on the front mat, and dodged under Mom's hand. "I'll check it out." Granddad used to be the man in the family. It was up to me now.

Mom grabbed the back of my shirt. "Stop! The burglar could still be inside."

My older sister, Melissa, pulled out her cell phone. She tapped her red-painted fingernail into the screen. Her brown, piercing eyes, which looked just like mine, darted between Mom and me. "I'll call the police."

I twisted away from Mom. "I can take care of things." I pretended to be a cop and strutted into the kitchen. I wasn't afraid. We didn't have anything anyone would want, anyway. I bet the burglar didn't stick around long.

In the kitchen, Granddad's old basset hound chewed

happily on a hunk of raw meat. He lay underneath a dirty white wall where a calendar with a picture of the Rochester falls running in a steady stream cascaded through the month of March. We never gave Mr. Pooch raw food because he had a small diarrhea problem, and he ruined the carpets with his doggie stains. Mom said we were never going to get the deposit back on the apartment. I didn't mention that the apartment manager didn't even know we'd inherited Grand-dad's dog. "Dog has a piece of raw meat!" I hollered.

"What?" Mom scurried into the kitchen toward Mr. Pooch. "Give me that!" She stuck out her hand.

I doubted Mr. Pooch was going to hand Mom his meat.

"Stay here!" I said in my deepest voice. "I'll scope out the rest of the apartment."

I stalked into the living room. The heavy, black curtains were still closed, blocking out the Rochester City recycling center. The curtains never did a good job keeping out the sound of the crunching glass and flattening cardboard machines. I grabbed the remote control and clicked on the buttons. We didn't have a flat-screen TV. We had one of the old-style big-box TVs. It worked most of the time.

"Everything looks good," I said. "The TV is still here and working." I couldn't really see robbers hauling away a TV that weighed more than my bed anyway.

"Don't touch anything!" Mom yanked the control out of my hands. "We want to get the crooks' fingerprints." She peered around the room and lowered her voice. "They might even still be here."

I shook my head and shrugged. "I doubt it." Mom had a flair for the melodramatic. Granddad tried to keep a lid on her drama by not encouraging her fear. I hoped to be like him, but at twelve I hadn't learned how to censor myself too well, something which my teachers and school counselor said caused trouble for me.

"The police are on their way." Melissa peered around the room. A strand of thin blond hair slipped out of her barrette and dropped into her eye. She pushed it out of the way. We shared the same type of hair, thin and scraggly. But Melissa tried to change hers with color treatments, straightening and curling. None of it worked, and the hair ended up in big gobs in our bathtub sink.

I turned and headed into my dining-room "bedroom." A few weeks ago, Melissa quit her job at the ski resort and moved home, but she didn't tell us why she left. After a heated discussion, Mom gave Melissa my room and I moved to the dining room. I stared at the empty place at the end of my bed.

"Mom!" I hollered. "Granddad's trunk is missing." A small, angry cloud rose inside me. The cloud promised to erupt into a storm. The storm threatened to grow so big it would rise up and out of the house and take over the entire block, the entire city, the entire state. Granddad gave the trunk to me before he died. It was the last thing he gave me, and now someone else had it. I blinked. I squinted. I rubbed my eyes. It didn't matter. The trunk with Granddad's antique toys was gone.

"The police are here," Melissa said, as she followed a tall, dark-haired man into the dining room.

"That was fast." Mom whirled around.

"I was around the corner. Your daughter said there's been a robbery?"

"Someone stole Granddad's trunk." I walked up to the officer and looked him in the eye. "You have to find it." I read the small, gold name tag on his blue vest. "Officer Tim."

Mom wiped her eyes with a balled-up tissue. "I'm sorry. We're a little upset. We were at my dad's funeral and now his trunk is missing."

"I'm sorry for your loss." Officer Tim pulled out a small notebook and pen from his pocket. "This sounds like an obit robbery."

"Who?" I tried to see what Officer Tim was writing, but he moved the notebook away from me. I crossed my hands across my chest and leaned back, studying Officer Tim as if he was a specimen in my science lab.

"Obit robberies," Officer Tim said. "Robbers find out when a funeral is held. They rob the family during the funeral. Did many people know your grandfather?"

"Everyone knew him! He invented the Springy Jig." Every year, Granddad's toy was voted the best summer toy by the Rochester toy shops. The waterfront shop always placed a big poster in their window. In the summer, Granddad brought a bag filled with his toys to the lake. He walked up and down the lakeshore beach and showed everyone how to toss it into the air so the springs released and it floated to the ground in a gentle swirl before landing with a slight plop, only to pop back up again and dance in the air like a kite. I loved helping Granddad. We picked out just the right kids to receive a toy for free. It was like playing Santa Claus in the middle of summer.

"Sorry." Officer Tim shook his head. "I haven't heard of him."

I scowled. "Maybe you know his house. At Christmas, Granddad set up Santa's workshop. He had the best light display on his street. I helped him string the lights." I swallowed the lump in my throat. Who would set up Granddad's Santa workshop this year?

Officer Tim shook his head. "I don't know that house."

I kicked a piece of the shaggy carpet. Who was this police officer and why didn't he know anything about Granddad? Everyone knew Granddad. Everyone!

"Can't you find these obit robbers?" Melissa asked. Her voice tilted upward in that polite tone she used for adults to get what she wanted. She perfected it in high school and easily won the contest for collecting the most donations every year in the canned-food drive. Even when I stood with her outside the grocery stores and handed out flyers printed with a list of items the food bank needed, I never could get anyone to pay attention to me, not like Melissa. Melissa oozed charm that made people want to do things for her. I had the opposite problem: no one wanted to do anything for me. Now I waited to see how Officer Tim would respond.

"We haven't been able to yet. The crimes have picked up all winter," Officer Tim said. He gave away no sign that he was swayed by Melissa. At his side, a walkie-talkie crackled. Officer Tim clicked a knob and it went silent. "I'll add this one to the list. If we hear something, we'll let you know."

"That's it?" The storm inside me gurgled. "That's all you're going to do?"

"Sorry, son," Officer Tim said. "We'll do the best we can and let you know if we find something."

I balled my fists. "If you can't find out who stole Granddad's toys, I will!"

Officer Tim turned and looked me in the eye. "Things aren't always what they seem," he said, and stepped out the broken door.

I picked up a cushion from the couch and hurled it at the wall. Things were exactly as they seemed. Granddad's toys were stolen.

CHAPTER TWO: SPAGHETTI

The next day it took a long time to bike home from school. The snow started falling during second-period math, and by two-thirty, fluffy layers covered the ground. I loved snow during the winter, but by March, I, along with everyone else, was tired of the enormous, gray slushy piles which lines the roadways and made riding my bike to and from school a chore. I was wiped by the time I chained the bike to the rack outside our apartment building.

The lock on the front door was still busted and I gave it a big shove to open. Mom sat on the living-room couch. Thursdays were Mom's nights off from the janitorial service. I always tried to give her a little space. "Hey, Mom." I tiptoed around the couch.

Mom glanced up at me and smiled. "Hey, Colt." Dark circles rimmed her eyes and her hair stuck up in places. She'd been sleeping on the couch since Melissa moved home a few weeks ago. Mom said their rooms were too close together and Melissa liked to talk on her cell phone and she wanted to give her space. I wasn't entirely sure that was the real reason. Mom hadn't been sleeping since Granddad died, and I often heard the TV playing into the wee hours of the morning.

Melissa hadn't found a new job yet and sat at the dining-room table, working on a resume. I didn't know why a resume was necessary. She hadn't worked at anything but coffee shops and I couldn't see how that would pay her part of the rent Mom insisted she contribute now that she was home again. I really wanted to know why she left her job at the ski resort, working in their fancy restaurant as a waitress. It was the first full-time job she'd landed since graduating from high school last spring and she only stayed three months. Ski season still had weeks to go before ending, and then she could have stayed for the summer hiking season. Mom tried every day to ask her about why she left, but Melissa kept repeating she was taking some time off to "find herself." I wondered why she was lost and how much time did it take to find your-self. I hoped not too much longer because I really wanted my room back.

Melissa waved a printed newsletter at me. "There's an art show at your school. Mom doesn't work tonight." Melissa tucked a strand of blond hair behind her ear. "We should all go see your art."

"I don't think that's a very good idea," I mumbled. I liked sixth-grade art class, but I had to be inspired. I liked to walk around the room and look at everyone else's art, but Ms. Richards didn't like walking around. She gave me one warning and then wrote passes to the counselor's office. Ever since I started middle school last fall, I spent a lot of time in the counselor's office, and very little time actually doing art.

"The art show is a great idea." Mom stepped into the kitchen. "I'd like to see your school work. You don't bring very much of it home."

"I'm hungry." I pulled open the refrigerator door and stuck

my head inside. I needed to think of a good reason why my art wasn't at the show.

"Why don't you pull out the package of hamburger meat?" Mom asked. "I'll make some spaghetti. It's your favorite."

Spaghetti. My stomach rumbled as I grabbed the meat. A ten-pound weight crashed into me: Granddad loved cooking spaghetti. Granddad always asked me to help chop up the green peppers and onions. Suddenly, I couldn't breathe. An elephant lay against my chest and wouldn't move.

"Colt?" Mom placed her hand on my back. "Are you okay?"

I yanked my head out from the refrigerator. "I'm not really hungry."

I scurried out of the kitchen and hustled into my dining-room bedroom. I wished for a door with a lock. From the kitchen, I heard Melissa say, "It's okay, Mom, just give him some space."

Score one for Melissa. I crash-landed onto my bed and lay flat on my back, staring at the ceiling. Where did someone go when they died? Could Granddad see me? Could he follow me around all day and see what I was doing? Was he in the bedroom with me right now?

Granddad had been sick for about a month before he died. They put him in a special rehab home. I went to visit him once, but he didn't look like Granddad. His face was gray and there were all these tubes sticking out of him. He didn't open his eyes when I was there. I didn't go back. I didn't want to remember Granddad on that bed.

I sat up and balled a fistful of blanket. I stared at the empty space at the end of the bed. After Granddad died, Mom said we could take a few things from his house to our apartment across town before Mom listed the house for sale. I loved Granddad's house. It had four bedrooms and a big loft as well as a large kitchen which always had good things cooking. We visited Granddad a lot, but never spent the night. Mom said the neighborhood wasn't good, but I never saw anything bad. Sometimes, Granddad said he wished we could move in and fill the empty bedrooms of Mom's childhood home, but Mom wouldn't even consider it. Whenever the subject came up, her lips closed up tight and her eyes narrowed. I guessed living next to the city recycling center was better than living in a bad neighborhood, whatever that meant.

The day we visited Granddad's house, I chose his trunk he kept in the living room and used as a coffee table. Mom and I hauled the old black trunk with fake-gold latches that didn't work very well upstairs to our apartment and opened it. Inside were backgammon and chess games. The tracks for Granddad's train set lay neatly linked together alongside metal train cars. Granddad always set up his train set at Christmas. I loved the car with the cat on the side of it. Granddad said it was the Chelsea Cat car. At the bottom of the trunk was a complete iron circus set, including a circus tent, elephants, and a girl who looked like she could swing on a trapeze. There were also several metal toys along with small cars and boats, which all looked very old.

Now I flipped onto my stomach, leaned down, and touched the floor where the trunk had been. Why would a thief want Granddad's toys?

To read more of Seymour's Secret check out your favorite bookstore.

Made in the USA
Columbia, SC
13 March 2023

13617301R00111